Baby Momma 2

Baby Momma 2

Ni'chelle Genovese

www.urbanbooks.net

Urban Books, LLC
78 East Industry Court
Deer Park, NY 11729

ISBN 13: 978-1-60162-538-0
ISBN 10: 1-60162-538-3

First Printing March 2013
Printed in the United States of America

10 9 8 7 6 5 4 3 2 1

This is a work of fiction. Any references or similarities to actual events, real people, living or dead, or to real locales are intended to give the novel a sense of reality. Any similarity in other names, characters, places, and incidents is entirely coincidental.

Distributed by Kensington Publishing Corp.
Submit Wholesale Orders to:
Kensington Publishing Corp.
C/O Penguin Group (USA) Inc.
Attention: Order Processing
405 Murray Hill Parkway
East Rutherford, NJ 07073-2316
Phone: 1-800-526-0275
Fax: 1-800-227-9604

Dedicated to Yvetta Tonia.

All too often we don't recognize the Angels that have been placed in our lives until they're gone . . .

Acknowledgments

It's funny because I used to complain about never getting any sleep, and now I never complain because it's my dream that keeps me awake. To the Creator of all things including this wonderful talent that I've been blessed with—I give God all the glory.

There was shock and awe the first time around and now I'm just happy knowing I've made you both so very proud—to my parents, Haywood and Cheryl Boyd, you set me loose into the world scared that I wasn't ready . . . and um I think it's safe to finally say it's the world that you should have been more worried about. I love you both so very very much.

My adopted big bro, mentor, manager, coconspirator, spiritual warfare counselor, financial advisor lol! You have too many titles for me to list them all! Maurice Tonia, I love you and thank you for the idea and the foundation that started it all—you made the impossible a possibility and then together we turned it into a reality.

My Sunshine Tiffany Wynn and My Smoochie Katey Kocsis I owe you both a world of thank-you's for all the inspiration, patience, and the distractions even when I should've been writing <3

Author Dahni McPhail, aka Dj Sporty—I've got so much love and respect for you, you are one of the most creative and multifaceted people I know and I'm happy to step aside and watch you take off, it's definitely

Acknowledgments

your time. Iisha, Pk Allday, Christie, Angel—thank you all for accepting me with open arms. I owe all of my Bruncher's a huge thank you for all the warmth and support, oh yeah and the crazy adventures.

Brandy V., Beverly H., Keshara, Stephanie P., Gwennetta aka my Gigi, y'all all kept me from going crazy in between those three walls of my cubicle on more than one occasion. Marie H., thank you all for your friendship and understanding. My literary agent, Joylynn, thank you for keeping me on track.

To my oh so supportive FB fam Lana, Eve, Detra, Velma, Terricka, Jina, Mrs. Stephanie H.L., Leslie H.J., Shatika, Jerrell, Elmyra, Dawnsheika, Marissa, Deirdra, Aray, Lanika, Shannon, Kristine, Anoosha, Brandi, Sonya, Penny, Shauna, Lakesha and the Diamond Divas Book Club, Keyiona and Angie B's Reading Between the Lines book club in Cincinnati. Everyone that's shown their support I <3 you all. Ni'chelle G.

Follow me on Twitter @NichelleG4.

Everything I do is for Jazmyn. Montre. Bryce. Asia. Kailah. Techa aka Westside Carman Ayala and Carol Mackey of Black Expression book club my two BFF for life. To all my sisters & FB friends: To Sissy Tonya Clay. Saran Day. Gwen. Cherly. Erica. LeQuisha. Brooke Taylor. Tia Pic. Mishelle. NiQua. Latoya. Glynnis Tasha Felder. Tracy Jeter. Renay. Mellissa. Latoya. Andrea, aka Miss Sunshine. Mocha. Connie. Helena. QuTasha. Carlene. Anza. Marissa Palmer. Jennifer of NJ. Pansy. Michelle Rawls. Jatoria, aka LuxHair. Adina. Tasha Powell. Renatta. Tara. Rashida Elisha, my Jersey sis. Shanell Red, one of the best songwriters in the world, thank U for all the advice. Darren Hicks & Tish, thank U. To my brothers. Governor. Moosh. Mark. TKO. Shawn Clay. Marysol, aka Ms Latin. Stephanie. Juilia McElligott. Tracey Jenkins. Albert. T-Black Big Mike.

Acknowledgments

Gary. Larry Jr. & Toya Tonia. To my wife, I don't need to say a word just "I Love You."

RIP Yvetta Tonia: When I thought God couldn't hear my voice, she prayed for me. When everyone turned their back, she stayed with me. When I failed, she stood for me. When I felt suffocated, she breathed for me. When I felt like nothing, I was her everything. *She is everything to me.*

An extra special thank you to the cast and crew of Baby Momma The Movie:

Techa Lewis, Malcom L Banks II, Michael Taylor Ross, Renatta Nicole Spann, Lennel Hall, Ben Lane, Nina McAlpin, Michael D. Ballard, Evelynn Danh Makanaakua, Deontae Marico Harris, Tia Cherrice, Essence Allen, and Victorye Pulliam.

PROLOGUE

"I hate this picture, Chelle; it look like I'm cock-eyed or somethin'."

We were sitting in first class, ready to start our flight from Virginia to Fort Lauderdale, Florida. Taking her driver's license from her I glanced at the photo, and handed it back. "You look fine, baby. Stop bein' so dramatic; ain't nothing wrong with that picture."

"Larissa Laurel. I do like our new last name though. It looks like I could be a model or a actress, some kinda shit you would see on the big screen. . . ." Her voice trailed off.

My mind wandered. It had been roughly three months since the day I'd visited Rasheed in prison to tell him what had happened and, after that, we'd packed up all of our shit and we were getting the hell out of Virginia for good. No looking back and no second thoughts. I glanced over to make sure the baby was still asleep, since we'd just taken off. I didn't want to be the woman with the loud-ass kids up in first class. She was unconscious, and Trey was busy with a pile of Goldfish—he'd be quiet until they disappeared.

I stared at my reflection in the window, my hazel eyes becoming part of one of the clouds and staring back at me. *Who am I?* Michelle Roberts—no, Michelle Laurel—a mother, wife, a heroine, or a monster . . .

"You ain't heard nothin' I been sayin', have you?"

I looked up. I couldn't lie; I hadn't heard a single thing. Ris could go on and on about any- and every-thing, and I zoned out so much it's a wonder she'd even talk to me sometimes.

"I'm sorry, baby, I was thinking about all the stuff we have to do once we get to the new house. You need a car, the kids need new clothes. I've got the new business starting up, and if this first buy goes through it could make it so neither of us has to work for anyone ever again, but then I'd have to start lookin' into staffing and building a client base—"

"Well I was *sayin'* we should decorate the house in Wang Chung." She rolled her eyes at me and popped her tongue.

I was looking at her like she was crazy, trying to interpret whatever the hell it was she'd misinterpreted, so I could figure out what she was talkin' about. I couldn't help laughing at her faux pas. "You wanna decorate the house in what? Don't you mean feng shui?"

"Ain't that what the hell I said? Anyway, I was lookin' at this show an' they was talkin' 'bout all the shit that it's good for like wealth an'. . ."

She went on like she hadn't heard anything that I'd just said.

I rubbed my eyes; they were feeling tired and dry from the hours of researching and reading I'd been doing over the last few weeks. I'd been busy starting my own real estate company on top of getting our shit packed and making sure everything went through with adopting the baby and having her name changed with our name changes. The prison was telling me the child's name was Paris and, um, I was not having that shit. La-taya Katrice Laurel was a beautiful name for a beautiful little girl and, since I'd always wanted a daughter, she was the perfect fit for our little family. From day one, I'd been treating her as if she were my own.

I couldn't wait to finally get to a place that we could call home that didn't have any bad memories, or a bunch of bad vibes attached to it. Everything in Virginia felt tainted in some way, shape, or form. We couldn't go eat at Rockafeller's because Rah used to take me there and Ris would get all types of jealous. Then, we'd have an issue over something simple and she'd say, "The only reason you ordered that is 'cause he always ordered that shit. Why you can't try somethin' different?"

My answer to that would be, "Maybe it's because I just like this shit and don't want anything different."

My statement would then be followed by Ris slamming down her menu and staring at me. Her eyes would have that "ready to fight" glow and she'd say, "Nah, I jus' think you miss that nigga."

And *bam:* a fight over something as simple as dinner.

We couldn't eat at IHOP because Rah used to take Honey, and Lord knows who else, up in there and then I would start to feel some kind of way, wondering which waitresses knew he was there with which skank. I knew I shouldn't think like that about Lataya's birth mother and call her a skank, God rest her soul. But still, it bothered me knowing some of those people there knew he had a family at home and not only watched him, but *encouraged* him in his bullshit; parading them hoes around town, fuckin' whichever one was the flavor of the moment. Yes, a change was definitely going to do the entire family some good.

I didn't tell Larissa that, as part of the surprise, I'd already had the house decorated but, maybe, we could take everything out of one room and decorate it "Wang Chung" style just for her. I giggled to myself again for that one, besides it was a big-ass house we would grow into. It was way too big for just the four of us right now but when I saw it I knew it was perfect. There was a playroom for the kids with this beautiful jungle mural painted on the walls and ceiling, with monkeys swinging from the trees and a giraffe. The kids would be in awe. I had a library that I couldn't wait to fill up with all kinds of books, and a pool to swim in. It had all that fancy shit that neither of us grew up with. We'd have it all from now on if I could help it and we both deserved it so much. My family wasn't going to want for anything because I planned on doing *everything* in my power to see us all well taken care of.

CHAPTER 1

HOME INVASION

(2 years later . . .)

Glancing down at my iPhone calendar, I checked my itinerary one last time. I could still show the Matthews property, finish up the paperwork, and make the forty-five-minute drive home in time for dinner. I pulled my all-black Lexus ES350 into the large circular driveway, careful not to scratch my rims on the damn rounded curb as I parked. Last time Larissa drove my car she curb-checked the hell out of the left side and I still cringed whenever I thought about what it cost to replace just two of those Lexanis.

The mansion loomed before me, picture perfect, like something straight out of a movie. Sand-colored cobblestone led the path toward the massive oak front doors. I grabbed up my things, deciding, instead, to take the long way around the back of the house. This way I could personally make sure the new landscaping company we were using was on point. It was the minor details that meant everything to the people who bought these types of homes and I had no intention of missing out on a major sale over a fuckery and bullshit minor technicality.

Everything looked in order. The hedges were trimmed into neat, identical squares and the thick carpet of lush green lawn was cut and edged beautifully. Small palms lined both sides of the large back yard overlooking the ginormous pool and Jacuzzi. It was early June and nearly eighty degrees out, and the water looked all too inviting. I didn't think I'd ever adjust to the difference between eighty degrees in Florida and eighty degrees in Virginia. My blouse was already starting to stick to my back from the humidity and the moisture in the air. At least in Virginia we had dry heat; this damp hotness was for the birds. I walked past a flowering bush. Its scent immediately reminded me of the Botanical Garden and instantly I knew why this was one of my favorite estates. It had that *Alice in Wonderland* kind of feeling, like at any moment a little rabbit wearing a Queen of Hearts jacket would come running out from in between the shrubs to offer me a drink. I laughed to myself. I wasn't sure exactly what it was but the place just felt like it could be home.

I let myself in through the back door into the kitchen. I paused mid-step, head tilted to one side. *What the hell?* I knew, too well, what it sounded like when a woman was gettin' the business, and Lord knows I heard what sounded like heavy breathin' and the soft telltale moans of a woman obviously lost in the type of passion that makes you not care who's listenin'. I gently laid my leopard-print Pineider Cavallino briefcase on the granite kitchen counter. My Mace was in a small, light brown leather clip attached to the side that slid off almost effortlessly. I removed it and silently made my way toward the sound.

Here I was, Gretel following a breadcrumb trail of hastily shed clothing. All these fairy tale analogies—whew, I'd definitely been reading way too many bedtime stories to the kids. Red pumps, Michael Kors loafers, black tube top, Rock & Republic jeggings; all items that led me from the kitchen down across the foyer to the double winding staircase. I was in stealth mode, creeping along on my toes, heels never touching the floor for fear of the click-clack alerting the intruders to my presence and ruining my element of surprise. I gripped my Mace tightly in my hand.

I was greeted at the top of the carpeted stairwell by a black and grey Burberry button down and Armani slacks. Somebody had good taste in clothes and by the sounds coming from the cracked door a few feet in front of me, it didn't stop there. My pulse quickened as I edged toward the door. Greedily my eyes took in the display of what a bitch can only describe as masculine perfection. Unconsciously, I licked my lips as I followed a trail of sweat that ran down his spine and pooled in the small of his back. For a moment I was lost in a voyeuristic fantasy. I could hear him accenting each pump with a word.

"Say. You. Want. This. Dick."

The nigga was workin' it. A dull ache started in between my own legs and my hand flew to cover my pussy out of some stupid fear that he'd actually hear it screamin' back, "I want it!" I couldn't see shit but two thin, stork-like legs poking out from either side of his hips, the black down comforter on the bed being so thick and all. I wouldn't have known there was a woman beneath him if it weren't for her pencil legs and loud porn star–sounding moans.

I hadn't been with a man sexually in what seemed like forever, maybe three years; hadn't looked at one, hadn't thought about one. Damn sure hadn't desired one—until now.

Months of faking and falling asleep unsatisfied had brought me to this moment. Ris and I were at that point where the spark was kinda gone out of our situation. My ass was bored. I was tempted to start moving my fingers. Use this as a chance to release all my pent-up frustration. I glanced down at my watch: 2:45 P.M. My three o'clock appointment would be here at any moment and I definitely had no time for this bullshit. I needed to straighten up the mess these fools were making before my client arrived. After one last longing gaze I straightened up my blazer, patted my bun, and stepped into the room, clearing my throat.

I wasn't sure what was more alarming: the fact that I was now no more than an arm's reach away, or that he looked directly at me and didn't even miss a stroke. I bit my lower lip. The nigga had the sexiest almond-shaped brown eyes. They glowed like golden coals against his dark skin. *Damn.* I was not expecting that. His eyes focused in on mine in an almost predatory manner. He visually drank me in and suddenly I was the recipient of each thrust. We were pretty much eye fuckin' right now for lack of anything else to call it. I felt parts of me start to awaken and throb in such a way that my ass was scared to keep watching and too damn fascinated to turn away.

The woman, now more clearly visible, seemed oddly familiar. Her head was thrown back, eyes closed tight in ecstasy. She was so thin and palely light skinned beneath his thick, muscular frame that it looked like he was splitting her in half. *Double damn!* Dazed, my nipples hardened beneath my blouse as he lowered his head and flecked his tongue across her barely there breasts, her physique embarrassingly boyish compared to mine. It was as if my body had a mind of its own and even though my brain was saying, *girl, go,* I was glued to the floor. My nostrils involuntarily flared and I felt myself slowly coming to life as blood rushed to my most sensitive parts. I could smell his sweat and her wetness, all mingling with the woodsy aroma of the $4,000 cherry nightstand in the corner that I'd just had unpacked yesterday, and *him.*

As if splashed with cold water my body jolted back to reality. I only knew *one* mu'fucka who wore Issey Miyake and now the scent alone brought to mind entirely too many bad memories. I snapped out of my daze and cleared my throat again, loudly this time.

"Excuse me, you need to get out of here before I call the police."

Hearing my voice, the woman sprang to an upright position, resting on her elbows, pulling the comforter up to cover herself. I recognized her almost immediately: Yylannia Besore. She was one of the hottest models out right now, half black and French, or something like that—I couldn't remember. But, I'd seen her a hundred times in the latest magazines and commercials. I couldn't believe she'd appear so boyish and lanky in person. She was nothing like the sexual vixen she appeared to be on camera but, lo and behold, I guessed that's what the wonders of makeup and Photoshop could do for a person.

"Where the fuck did *she* come from?" Yylannia was trying to untangle herself from the statuesque man who had her pinned in place.

He sat back on his haunches with a sigh of frustration and obvious resentment at my intrusion, allowing her to scamper off the bed and quickly dart past me to grab her things and get dressed.

My eyes molested him from the neck downward. Huge pecs lightly dusted with soft, straight dark hair that narrowed into a thin line as it ran downward in between tight abs and . . .

"You couldn't have waited jus' li'l bit longer huh?"

I jerked myself back to reality. My head whipped up so fast I was surprised it didn't make the snap noise like in one of those old-school kung fu movies. His voice was deep, unbelievably deep. It sounded like warm honey to my ears.

"No, and you need to put some fire to ya ass an' get outta here before I call the police."

The cologne he wore made me dislike him immediately. But his sex appeal was making my psyche do a double take. He reminded me of a large cat as he fluidly uncoiled himself from the bed. *Sway-backed nigga.* The curve in his lower back was so over-pronounced and the muscles in his ass so tight and high the image of a gorilla came to mind. He was thick as hell and sexy as fuck. Right about now, I could use a good gorilla fuck. I almost laughed out loud at the thought. Lord, I was definitely trippin'. He was a dark chocolate version of Leonidas from that movie *300*. My son, Trey, must have made me watch that movie a million times, and the only reason I could sit through it over and over again was because of all the beautifully built men who'd be on the damn TV screen.

Oh yes, he could've definitely passed for an ancient Spartan warrior. He had straight black hair, a Caesar low cut, long, thick sideburns that tapered beneath his chin into a thick, full beard. It highlighted the fullness of his pink lips and gave him an almost dangerous appeal. He picked his boxers up from beside the bed and slid them on. I tried not to smile because, despite my intrusion and threats, he was still standing at full, and I mean *full,* attention. Damn, it had to be painful for him to try to restrain all that behind nothing but a little tight wall of cotton.

"So, let me take a guess. You must be Michelle right?"

My eyes widened in surprise at the sound of my name flowing from Leonidas's beautiful, made-for-pussy-licking lips. *Whew.* I needed to calm down. *How does this fool know my name?*

"Um, yes. And who might you be?" Suspicion immediately made my tone sharp; I couldn't imagine anyone who looked like him actually knowing me.

"Key! I'ma go wait in the damn car!" Yylannia shrieked from somewhere downstairs.

Suddenly, I didn't need an answer. He was Keyshawn Matthews, the superstar rookie drafted to play for Miami. I hadn't noticed how exceptionally tall he was but I now felt dwarfed standing across from him, and I was close to five feet eleven without heels. I could feel my cheeks starting to get hot; my grown ass actually started blushing.

"Mr. Matthews? I . . . I am so sorry. I had no idea you even had a key to view the property. I guess you, um, you like it?" Here I was talking to one of the richest and probably most famous men in the NBA, and he was standing in nothing but his drawers! Ris was definitely not gonna believe this shit. *Oh hell, best to not even tell Ris; she'd probably get jealous and start trippin' any damn way.* He flashed me a dazzling white smile displaying perfect deep dimples and straight white teeth.

"Yeah, I was testin' the place out. My agent got me the key earlier. I parked in the garage. I'm lovin' all the space but the acoustics in this mu'fucka ain't right."

I raised an eyebrow, immediately puzzled. I had no idea what acoustics meant outside of a home theatre or studio. What did acoustics have to do with . . . "Wait, acoustics?"

I knew this nigga wasn't saying what I thought he was saying. The house we were in was one of the most sought after and high priced on the market. Fridays were my busiest days and I'd turned down two other closings and come out to show the property personally because Key's agent swore up and down he wanted to buy and close today. I owned High Rise Estates, the second-largest real estate agency in Fort Lauderdale, and I *only* came out to do closings. Most of our clients were usually in the market for their third or fourth vacation home and I left the aggravating task of showing property after property to the finicky doctors, starlets, and athletes in the area to my staff.

"Yeah, the acoustics is on some mute 'n' shit. I like to *hear* how good it feels when I'm puttin' in work. Jus' somethin' that's important to me. You wouldn't understand though. So, what's next?"

I stared in disbelief. This was that minor detail fuckery and bullshit I mentioned earlier. This fool done lost his damn mind if he was thinking I was gonna let him run his ass through house after house, fuckin' in staged bedrooms and messing up designer linens! I was on the verge of puttin' him on full blast, potentially losing a client and a sale, but I was saved by my iPhone, which had started ringing downstairs.

"I need to get that. You might wanna go ahead an' put your damn clothes back on in the meantime." Turning with a look of pure disgust, I rushed downstairs to answer my phone.

"Hi, Ris. Everything okay?" I breathed heavily into the phone.

"Hey, bae. E'rething's good. Why you breathin' so hard? What you doin'?"

"Nothing, I'm showing a property. Ran to grab my phone."

"Oh, well, when you comin' home so I know when to have dinner ready?"

I couldn't believe she was calling me during a showing to ask something like this. "Ris. Same time I always get home. Five-ish. Why, do you need me to pick somethin' up?" I was trying to make the convo quick since Keyshawn had just walked into the kitchen to put on his shoes. I didn't want him eavesdropping on my conversation. I pressed the volume down on the side of the phone just as Ris gave away the real reason for her call.

"Chelle, we need to talk when you get here. I jus' got this feelin'. I mean . . ."

Damn, here we go again. I could feel the aggravation creeping up the back of neck, causing my teeth to clench. Every other day Larissa seemed to "have a feelin'."

"Larissa, I will call you when I'm on my way home. I don't have time to talk about this with you again." I softened my tone in an attempt to soothe her. "I'm showin' a property right now, baby. Okay?"

She sighed loudly and was quiet for a moment before speaking. "Okay. I love you—my wife."

Damn it. She *only* did that wife shit when she thought I was talking around someone else. "I luh you too. My wifey." I tried to say it as quickly as possible but I knew he'd heard.

I ended the call and silently cursed. She was really driving me crazy with all her insecurities. Every time I left the house, or needed to run an errand, she was overly paranoid about me cheating on her, or going to meet someone else. Marrying her hadn't changed a thing; if anything it seemed like it'd made things worse.

"Damn, lemme find out yo' fine ass into chicks." Keyshawn was leaning on the kitchen counter with his chin in his hands, like we were best friends hanging out on a summer afternoon, talking over martinis.

I would have been mad at him listening if he weren't flashing the most beautiful smile in my direction, dimples and all. In that moment my heart skipped a beat and my body secretly, against my free will, betrayed my wife. I glanced at my watch and then back at the nigga in front of me, who was unknowingly making me grind my teeth and do my Kegels at the same time.

"An' happily married, Negro. Don't try to change the subject. So you don't want this estate now, huh?" I couldn't help feeling drawn into his playful manner and I leaned on the counter opposite him, mimicking his posture. "If you *really* knew how to make a woman scream, acoustics would be the least of your worries, playboy." I flashed a dazzling smile back in his direction and we shared a laugh.

"Ma, I promise, married or not, no woman can take you where a nigga can. I ain't talkin' 'bout no bullshit-ass plastic dick. I'm talkin' flesh and blood. It ain't the same. An' the acoustics, FYI, is to maximize the sound in the bedroom *without* wakin' up my houseguests or neighbors."

I mentally shook my head at myself. That actually shut my ass up. I didn't even have a comeback. The way Ris would let go and wake up the kids made me think about looking into soundproofing for my damn self. He was both disarming and charismatic. This was dangerous. I had a business to run, and if this fool wasn't making me any money he definitely wasn't worth my time.

"Well, I'll have one of my realtors follow up with you and offer several other properties that may better suit your standards, Mr. Matthews. In the meantime, I would suggest you inspect the properties clothed and in a respectable manner. Oh, and should the issue arise, jus' invest in soundproofing *after* you acquire the property, sir." I grabbed my things and approached the front door, intent on getting away from this man and his magnetic pull as fast as humanly possible. My hand was on the latch but the door wouldn't budge.

"What if I only wanna deal wi'chu?"

I hadn't even heard him come up behind me. His voice cascaded down the back of my neck in heated waves that coursed down my body and crashed into the ocean between my legs. Goosebumps rose on my arms and time seemed to stand still as his question floated between us. His hand was planted firmly on the door just above my head; no wonder I couldn't pull it open. He was so close behind me. I could feel a wall of heat along the back of my body as he leaned over me, waiting for my answer, expecting me to react like every other woman who had probably given in to his good looks and sex appeal.

"My wife is crazy as hell, and I think you've got enough on your plate to keep you occupied. I have police-grade Mace. Move, or I'll use it." I held my breath, silently wishing this were a different time, or I were a different me. He was a ride I couldn't afford to take right now.

Reluctantly, his hand slid from the door. I heard him take a step back.

"Ol' girl out there, she ain' nothin' but arm candy. But you, you naturally beautiful wit' all that real hair. Yeah, I can tell, an' I appreciate it. Your wife got e're right to be crazy, 'cause I honestly don't think you into that dikin' shit a hundred percent. I'll see you soon, Michelle."

CHAPTER 2

HOME GROWN

I was bored outta my damn mind. Chelle was always at work or wherever doin' who- or whatever and I was stuck up in here all day every day with the damn kids. The two of them were runnin' around the house, actin' like they were losin' they damn minds, fighting over every single solitary thing. There was nothing for me to do and I was gettin' restless as hell and the kids were startin' to work my damn nerves. I threw down the magazine I was trying to read, only making it half-way through the article on how to tell if your man was cheating. No, I ain't had no man. I just switched all the "if he's" doing this or that et cetera shit to "if she's," and damn if Michelle wasn't fitting the descriptions to a muthafuckin' T.

Lately she'd been working late with special clients on special closings, or taking longer to get home than usual. When we made love—hell I couldn't even call it that—it was more on some "I serve you until I'm bored, okay switch, now you do me" boring-ass shit. Nothing like when we first got together. Everything that damn magazine said was exactly what was going on in our house. *An' I be givin' her ass every opportunity to just tell me she seeing someone else but, like a mutha-fuckin' nigga, she refuse an' claims nothin's up.* You know how that shit goes. Deny, deny, deny 'til you die type shit. She could probably get caught in the act, dick or pussy in her mouth, ass, or whatever, and still be like, "Baby, it ain't what you think."

Pain shot through my foot; glancin' down, I got even more pissed off as I pulled one of Trey's Legos from underneath it. "Trey, stop chasin' yo' fuckin' sister an' come pick up these damn toys. I done told you 'bout leavin' these damn things all ova' the fuckin' place. I'ma start throwin' 'em away. Try me, li'l nigga." I stared his li'l lazy ass down while he picked 'em up slow as hell one by fuckin' one.

I did not sign up for this shit. I needed to be doing something with myself, running a business, keeping my mind busy earning myself some damn money. I hated dependin' on Michelle for every damn dime I wanted to spend. If it wasn't for the fact that we were basically in a self-induced witness protection program I could easily go out an' get myself some kind of work, but it was just easier if we kept people out of our shit. Daycares, constant babysitters, they all had questions and needed more info than she or I wanted to give.

I needed to talk to a damn adult. All this kiddy shit was getting to my ass. I pulled my cell out of my back pocket and called my cousin back home in Detroit: the only person I trusted.

"Girl, what da fuck you ova' there doin'?" I asked playfully as soon as she picked up. I was jus' glad she ain't let me go to voice mail. When we left Virginia, Michelle insisted we cut everyone off, but I couldn't let my entire family jus' think I'd off and died or disappeared. My cousin, Shanice, was the only person I trusted enough to still keep in contact with.

"Hey, boobie, I miss yo' li'l crazy ass. You lovin' dat married life yet?" She was being sarcastic as usual. She always was a smart ass.

"I don't even wanna go into the details. I think she seein' that muthafucka again or a new somebody. I ain't figured it out yet, but when I do it's gon' be on."

"Larissa, you ain't marry dat bitch jus' to have her doin' all the same shit. Check her ass, fo' I come out there an' check her for you. Paper or no paper all that extra shit ain't worth it."

I sighed into the phone; she had a point. It wasn't worth it and I knew it. After all of these years of loving Michelle and only Michelle it was finally starting to break me down. It's like how they say a tiny stream of water can eventually wear down a mountain until there's nothing left but a flat piece of land and a river. Well my love at one point was that mountain but all these doubts and fears been wearin' and tearin' away at that mountain for so long that we were on the verge of bein' completely torn apart and wiped away.

"Shanice, you've known me my entire life. I think this the longest my ass eva' been straight-up, flat-out sober. Hell, I don't even drink like that no more. The stress an' these kids, all this shit is startin' to get to me."

"Bitch, a blunt ain't neva' hurt shit. My ass ain't neva' heard of a mu'fucka bitin' nobody face off 'cause they was smokin' on some purp'." She was talkin' 'bout the recent drug shit that'd happened down in Miami. Niggas snortin' bath salts or whatever and eatin' other nigga's faces and brains *while the nigga was still alive* on some for real zombie-type shit.

"Girl, I tried to tell Michelle we need to get our asses the fuck up outta here before da Zombie Apocalypse start, an dat heffa told me stop watchin' da damn horror channel. You an' me bof know—don't *no* black folk do no shit like that, an' especially not off no damn weed. Hell, you don't even do nothin' close to that off a bad crack rock."

"True, bitch, *that is so got-damn true,*" Shanice yelled in my ear in agreement and we both fell out laughin'.

Most of my life I'd had a problem with various drugs from crack to cocaine, you name it. Michelle was on some warden-type shit right now. I could barely sniff a glass of wine without her looking at me sideways, getting all weary and talkin' to me in her "house nigga" voice. I could hear saying, "Look nah, Risi-cup, you done made it dis far now, an' ya knows what dey says 'bout stayin' strong an' takin' one day at a time."

Ugh.

"You ever grow that Chia Pet I sent yo' ass?" Shanice was gigglin' in the phone like a straight-up little girl.

"Girl, what da hell I'ma do wit' a damn . . ." I stopped, realizing what she was saying before I could even finish my sentence. "Shanice, you didn't."

"Yup. Dat last package I sent you. Li'l Mr. Ch-Ch-Ch-Chia had a present inside his ass. I hope yo' ass ain't throw him away."

I didn't think I'd felt this damn happy the entire time I'd been in Florida. I'd gone to the post office one day and set myself up a post office box so I could have things shipped without my "warden" all in my business. I laughed and thought the Chia Pet was cute when I saw it.

"Girl, I go'sta go. Hell naw, I ain't throw it away, it's somewhere in the damn garage. Hell Ch-Ch-Ch-Chy-eah!" I rushed my black ass off the phone so fast I ain't even say bye.

"Trey, Taya, go lay y'all's asses down, it's damn nap-time," I shouted up toward their playroom, satisfied when I heard the pitter-patter of they bad asses run-ning to get in their beds. I needed to figure out exactly where the hell I'd stuck that damn package because apparently it had some extra shit up in it and I *needed* that in my life right now. It would be easier to figure out how I was going to talk to this woman, aka my so-called wife, about this new shit that popped up in our situation if I was at least a little lifted.

CHAPTER 3

JUST A FRIENDLY REMINDER

Traffic was backed up on the I-95 expressway in both directions. Cursing to myself I dialed the house phone. Something told me I should've just gone straight home after meeting with Key. It was already going on six and Larissa was probably jumping to all kinds of conclusions. Times like this made me miss Virginia; at least there I could hop on the midtown or downtown tunnel and be home in twenty minutes, or get off on any of the side streets and still be there like it was nothing. Not here; I had to cut clear across town to get back home, and this shit this time of year with the tourists and the locals trying to get in and out of town was insane.

"Hey." She picked up and that one word said it all: short and shitty mad.

"Baby, I'm stuck in traffic on the highway. I had to drop the contract off back at the office. You won't believe who—"

"No, Michelle, *you* won't believe what it's like stuck up in this house all damn day wit' two kids waitin' on somebody to bring they ass home when they say they will. What da hell happened to 'five-ish'? You know what, don't even answer dat. I'll just see you when you get here." Silence.

Did she just? Yes, her ass did. Chelle, calm down.
Edging through traffic, I gave myself a pep talk. I was

on the verge of walking up in that seven-bedroom, $3,000-a-month mortgage house and goin' slam the fuck off. I alone paid that mortgage and upkeep on that house her unappreciative ass was suddenly so upset about being "stuck up in all day." Shit, it's not like she didn't have a car. Larissa had two cars. Why she refused to leave the house without me by her side was just another argument waiting to happen.

Forty-five minutes later I parked in front of our garage and braced myself as I walked in through the front door. Even the short distance from the car to the front door broke me out in a mild sweat and the AC gave me an instant chill when I walked in. Normally when I got home from work my babies' little arms would wrap around my legs. Trey and Lataya, my four-year-old son and two-year-old adopted daughter, would squeal and giggle as I play tugged, dragged, and scuffed up freshly waxed hardwood flooring and let them put runs in my brand new stockings, but the house was dead silent. I walked through the foyer into the living room. The curtains were drawn against the setting sun, casting the room in warm shadows.

"A'ight. So, where was you really at?" Her tone was half asking and half accusatory.

I stopped in the entryway. For a brief moment I was alarmed. Was she using again? Was she high on something right now? No, that wasn't possible. I could clearly hear the shakiness and the tears in her voice. After we'd gotten married and gained legal custody of Lataya, the daughter of her cousin Honey and my ex-fiancé, Ris had managed to stay away from all that shit, just like I'd managed to avoid dick. I erased the negative thought just as soon as it occurred.

"Ris, I told you. I had to show the Matthews property an' drop off the paperwork. You know how traffic is this time of year."

She was sitting off in a darkened corner of the living room with her legs drawn up to her chest, chin resting on her knees. Times like this, I exhaled long and hard. It was the times like this that she reminded me of the old hurt and emotionally worn down me. Except I wasn't intentionally putting her through half the shit I was actually going through back then. I walked toward her slowly with the same cautious, timid approach you'd take with a hurt bird or injured deer, scared to move too quickly out of fear that she'd dart upstairs and lock herself in the bathroom and I'd be stuck outside the door for the rest of the night trying to talk her out.

"C'mon, you. Now, what's the one thing I said I'd never do?" My voice was nothing but a low whisper. My emotions were getting the best of me and my own tears slowly started to trail down my cheeks at the sight of her obvious pain.

"I know wha'chu said, Chelle. But, you're you, an' you're smart an' beautiful an' I jus' don't see you lovin' me forever. Not like you try to say you will. Nothin', not a damn thing, last forever, an' I rather you jus' be honest wit' me an' say you gonna do some shit or dat you *are* doin' some shit than play me for a damn fool."

The sun was setting and tiny slits of light were peeking through the thick chocolate-colored drapes that covered the ceiling-to-floor windows in the living room. It was just enough light for me to briefly see dark shadows underneath my wife's usually bright green eyes. Ris always kept herself up but she was still in her thin pink cotton slip from the night before, her long, shoulder-length red hair was piled up in a messy-ass ponytail on top of her head. It was enough for me to realize that she was seriously worried and all for nothing. God knows I hated when she acted like this. I wasn't cheating on her and hadn't thought about it. *Ugh.* Inwardly I cringed. Okay, until *today* I hadn't actually thought about cheating on her. But, let's be real, that wasn't an actual, tangible thought until I had it swinging in my damn face. Let's be honest, it was more of what I'd consider a fleeting whim. A fantasy. Nothing more, nothing less.

"Risi-cup, you'll never enjoy the moments life has to offer if you stay focused on the ending." I recited some psychobabble I'd read or heard somewhere, and dropped down to my knees in front of her, offering up what I'd hoped would look like a reassuring smile.

"It ain't workin', Chelle. Not this time." She handed me a crumpled piece of paper.

"What's this, baby?" *Did I forget to pay the water bill or something crazy? Is that what has her so upset?* Puzzled, I took the crumpled sheet of paper from her cold hand and started to unfold and smooth it out as best as I could. It was a tattered piece of notebook paper; the words hit me to my core. Chills ran through my body and it took my mind a second longer to process what my heart almost immediately comprehended. The sheet of paper was wrinkled as if it'd been folded and refolded, balled up, thrown away, and found again, but the letters were still there—in what I guessed would have to be the worst handwriting I'd ever seen—but the blotchy red ink spelled it out unmistakably clear:

A FAMILY DIVIDED WILL FALL THE FUCK APART

Out of all the possibilities, I'd rather this shit be the sick joke of one of our neighbors. That would have been much easier to stomach. Ris and I were the only same-sex couple in the neighborhood and I could deal with a pissed-off "Jesus Freak" like it was nothin'. Yet my subconscious was raising flags redder than the words in front of my face. I looked up at Ris, who now had fresh tears welling up in her eyes, and only one name came to my mind.

"Did that nigga come here? Was he here? Who left this note? Did you see who left this?" I had a million and one questions. None of which Ris could answer fast enough. My mind was going a hundred miles an hour. There was no way he could be out of jail. No way he could have possibly known how to get to us. I changed my last name, changed the kids' last names. A sense of despair came over me that I fought with all of my being for the sake of my kids alone. Maybe he paid one of his old dope boys to follow us, but the types of men Rasheed dealt with didn't leave little notes, or calling cards, or any evidence. They handled business, got the fuck out of town, and you'd be lucky if they even left a body for your family to bury when they were done.

"I was takin' out the trash last week, an' it was on the back gate." She broke out into fresh tears.

"Last week? And you're just *now* showin' me this." I smacked the offensive sheet of paper in frustration. "Then, what the hell are you even cryin' for? I'm the one in shock right now, *you've* had a whole week to marinate with this shit."

"I thought that maybe y'all were meetin' up or somethin' since you were comin' home late or whatever blah blah bullshit. I been waitin' for the right time to say somethin."

I couldn't help rolling my eyes at her dumb-ass logic. "An entire week, Ris? Who knows who's been watchin' us. Watchin' you and the kids, me. Ris, I swear. . . ." My voice trailed off. I'd never put my hands on her in anger, but I swear this one time almost pushed me to my limit. I silently prayed for strength and some kind of restraint to keep from shaking her for being so damn stupid.

Ris was obviously under a ton of stress, but for her to think that I'd be seeing Rasheed again after all this time . . . Well, considering my and Rah's on-again, off-again history, I couldn't blame her. Her reaction was expected. Hell, I'd be a little suspect about me too if the roles were reversed. Our entire relationship was based on Larissa putting me back together every time Rasheed broke me down. It took years of me dealing with him lying and cheating to finally realize that I loved me too much and Ris loved me all along.

"Ugh, I need to think." Closing my eyes, I rubbed my temples, trying to process exactly what this message might mean. "Have you noticed any cars around the house or any strange people since the day you found this note?"

"No. I mean . . . Well I've noticed strange things about you. But—"

"Larissa, I swear on my life I ain't doing anything wrong. I need you to fuckin' focus right now. Where are the kids?" If there was any time for me to "woosah" or "nam-myoho-renge-kyo" meditate and chant, now was it. Out of all the things we needed to worry about concerning my ex and our past I couldn't believe she was still more worried about whether I was cheating.

Rasheed was supposedly in prison in Virginia, serving at least a full life term with no hope of probation. He'd lost everything: his family, his freedom, his businesses, hundreds of thousands of dollars. All because of the two of us.

"The kids upstairs takin' a nap."

Relief momentarily swept through me. At least my babies were in the house and they were safe. I could feel a migraine coming on. I'd have to get in contact with my attorney; there was no way in hell Rah could have found us on his own. I leaned in and hugged Ris, trying to reassure her as best as I could. She was rigid and didn't return my embrace. Pulling back, I looked at her, praying there was nothing more to go with her story.

"Baby. It'll be okay, I promise. Stop worryin'."

But it wasn't worry that I saw in her eyes, it was anger. Glowing, green anger. I was confused. Her face could have been carved out of stone it was so cold and still. Her eyes narrowed into cold green slits, and it was a wonder she could even see me. But I knew that look entirely too well; it meant hell was coming.

"If you weren't wit' da nigga, why you smell like him, Michelle?"

Fuck. Fuck was the first and only word that came to mind. *Fuck Keyshawn and his damn cologne and his damn advances and Ris's sensitive-ass nose. Fuck and double fuck.* She was staring at me so calmly it was scaring the hell out of me. She was gauging my reaction time, watching my pulse, waiting to see if I stuttered or fucked up my answer. The fucked-up part was I was more nervous about all the shit I knew she watching for and I didn't even do anything to deserve the interrogation I was getting.

"Ris, I told you I had to show that mansion today. Keyshawn Matthews, he plays basketball for the Miami Legends. I closed the deal. We hugged; his girlfriend was there I hugged her too. I called you on my way home to tell you that we're all goin' out to celebrate this weekend, like celebrities. The estate was ten million; it's a *huge* deal for us. I wanted you to be proud of me. And yes, he wears that same funky-ass cologne as Rah. I noticed it too. But that's it; nothing more, nothing less." I could see the wheels spinning, judging my words as true or false, and I must've said everything the right way because her face started to light up with excitement.

"Wait, the rookie 'Keys to the City Shawn' Matthews?"

I shook my head yes.

"The one who goes everywhere with Yylannia the supermodel?"

Once again all I could do was shake my head in agreement, slightly amazed that Ris, A, knew who they were and, B, actually seemed to be impressed.

"Chelle, they were all ova' all the celebrity blogs las' week. Dat fool be up in clubs throwin' thousands at crowds. Bae, he be goin' in. I ain' partied or had a real night out since . . . Ugh. What am I gonna wear? I gotta go shoppin'. We need a babysitter!" She jumped up off the couch so fast she almost knocked me over.

"Oh an' you need a shower. You think you can ask him not to wear dat stank-ass cologne when we go out? Tell his ass I'm allergic to it or some shit, ount care." She took off upstairs in a flurry, mumbling the names of clubs and drinks, dresses and who knew what else.

Lord, forgive me for the lie I just told. I'll never tell another one, just please let Key be available this weekend. But, something tells me as soon as I say the words "go on a celebration date with me and my wife," that fool's schedule will most likely miraculously clear up.

CHAPTER 4

I'LL SCRATCH YOUR BACK—
IF YOU SCRATCH MINE

I waited until Ris left the house to go shopping, making her take both my Mace and the .22 with her just to be safe. Surprisingly the kids were still down for their nap so the house was nice and quiet. Naptime meant playtime so they probably hadn't actually fallen asleep until just before I'd gotten home. I peeked in just to make sure they were still breathing. I guess it's a momma thing, but as long as I could see their little faces and hear the ever-so-beautiful sound of their even breathing, I knew everything was fine and I could go about my business. I grabbed my iPhone out of my briefcase and walked into our bedroom, which was a complete mess, as usual. Clothes were everywhere, on the floor, all over the king-sized bed. The doors to both walk-in closets were wide open, and Tornado Ris had blown through, leaving shoes and whatnot every damn where. I hated all the clutter and mess. She was so bad when it came to that shit, but I had too much on my mind to start picking up after her as I usually did.

I walked up the winding wooden staircase that was secluded off to the corner. It led up to the third floor, or what I liked to call my personal sanctuary. When I furnished the house I wanted one room that would be no one's but mine. I opted to make the small corner studio my home office instead of using the study downstairs as most of the homes were traditionally set up.

There was one large rectangular window that ran the entire length of the room, overlooking our view of the pool and beach beyond. Thin white drapes hung from either side and with the window open the breeze would carry the smell of the ocean. Every time I looked out at the ocean I couldn't help thinking that I had my very own piece of paradise right in my backyard. This was the only area of the house that I allowed white in. I didn't want to deal with the hassle of keeping little fingerprints off my furniture, so everything else in the house consisted of dark earth tones: chocolates, olives, and tans. Everywhere except my sanctuary. The floor was covered in the softest carpeting I could find, the color was called shaved ice, and that's exactly what it looked like. My desk was made completely out of glass and sat in the center of the window; my executive-edition plush white leather chair was just as I'd left it. Across from that on the other side of the room sat my white microfiber couch and sectional.

Lying back on the sofa, I kicked off my pumps. For a moment I just stared at the little clownfish—or the "Nemo's" as the kids called them—swimming around in the hanging tropical fish tank on the wall. *Oh well,* I thought. *Here goes nothing, or better yet here goes hell to pay if I can't pull this off.* I dialed Key's number. I didn't realize I was holding my breath until his voice mail came on and I was forced to breathe so I could leave a message.

"Um. Hi, Key. This is Michelle, from the house earlier. I need a huge favor. I'd really appreciate it if you'd give me a call back, hopefully tonight. Thanks." *Great, what the hell am I gonna do if this nigga doesn't call me back? Think, girl. Think.* I could feel the stress knots in my neck, and I closed my eyes and tried to come up with some kind of a backup plan just in case. I must have dozed off because the phone rang and scared me so bad I jumped. *About damn time.* "Keyshawn, hey."

"Well, well. You find me anotha house already?"

Damn, he ain't listen to his voice mail. Typical.

"Umm. No, I actually need a huge favor."

"Ha, okay, I'm listenin'.'"

"Well, remember when I said my wife was crazy? I got home stupid late from our showing an' she was spazzin' so I had to kind of lie about closin' on the house with you. I said we'd be goin' out tomorrow to celebrate."

"So, lemme guess. You want me to get us a table somewhere and chill wit' y'all right?"

"You *and* Yylannia, yes. I can knock maybe twenty percent off of whichever house you decide to close on or maybe throw flat screens in every room, work on that acoustic thing you were so interested in." I was trying to think of any- and everything to get him to commit. Even if he just showed up for an hour, played his part, and left. As long as Ris was happy and my life went back to normal I didn't care.

"How 'bout this? We do a date for a date. I chill wit' you an' wifey, an' say this time nex' week I treat you like you should be treated and take you out for dinner, drinks?" I could hear him smiling through the phone, dimples and all. He had me. There was no way I could say no, *but,* I could always cancel on his ass at the last minute.

"Fine, whatever. I heard LIV in Miami is next to impossible to get into wit' this late of a notice, but do you think you could get a table? I'll cover all the—"

"Woman, I don't need you coverin' nothin'. I'll have my man handle all the details, text me ya info an' I'll send a car to pick y'all up. We gonna do this big, since we celebratin' an' shit." He laughed into the phone. His moods were so contagious. It was nice to have someone else take over things, handle the arrangements and all the details.

"Thank you, Keyshawn. Guess I really do owe you one."

"Chelle? You up there?" Larissa was making her way upstairs. I imagined she'd either exhausted herself trying to find something to wear or maxed out another one of my cards. I made a mental note to check all of my balances and pay them all off at the end of the month.

"Yeah, baby. I'm here. All right, Key. Lemme go. I'll send you what you need. Thanks again." I hung up before I could hear a reply, and dropped my phone into my lap.

"Who were you talkin' to?" She stopped just shy of the edge of the stairs and looked at me suspiciously.

"Keyshawn. I was confirming our arrangements for tomorrow and making sure we have a sitter. Did you find a dress?"

She beamed a smile at me and launched herself into my lap. Her small four-foot-nine frame fit so perfectly with mine. Wrapping my arms around her, I couldn't help but roll my eyes. I already knew what she was going to say.

"Yes, I found us *both* dresses. 'Cause you know you ain't got shit to wear either, not to no damn club anyway."

"Ris, you know good an' well you can't shop for me. It's either gonna be too short, too tight, or too damn bright. I'm sure I already got somethin' in my closet that'll work."

"Nah, you'll like this shit. I promise." She leaned her head back on my shoulder and smiled up at me, making me momentarily forget that somewhere out there my crazy ex-fiancé was stalking us and that in all actuality we really weren't celebrating anything this weekend except for a lie I'd told her—and now I owed a date to man I was entirely too attracted to, to even admit to myself. I planted as fake of a smile on my face as I possibly could, and I leaned down, kissing her smiling lips, pretending as if nothing was wrong.

Saturday was a whirlwind of getting the kids ready for their day with the babysitter and trying to get my house back in order from a busy workweek. I'd noticed an older blue Ford Mustang in the neighborhood earlier. It went around the neighborhood once when I was checking the mail, and I was going to let Trey and Lataya play outside when I started to feel uneasy and decided against it.

"Mommy, why?" Trey whined. *My poor babies.* I felt bad keeping them cooped up in the house but it was for their own good. I looked down at Trey, who was getting so tall he was almost up to my waist. He was his father's same exact high-yellow complexion, lighter than me with pretty, curly hair and big, round brown eyes. I couldn't hide my smile as I answered him.

"Because Mommy says no, that's all the why you need."

Lataya stood beside him in a pink shorts set, white sandal on one foot and Lord knows where the other one was, looking like a miniature golden version of her mother if you let Ris tell it. When I looked at my little princess all I saw was Rasheed.

I knelt down to take off her sandal, frowning at a red welt on the back of her chubby little leg. She was in that terrible-twos stage, always stumbling around the house and getting into everything; it was probably nothing. Her front teeth were just starting to come in and she looked just like Trey when he was that age: all cheeks, slobbery chin, grinning all day for no reason whatsoever. She was such a happy little girl. I couldn't imagine the life she'd have had if we'd let her go to a foster home. She was so much better off here with us. This was definitely where she belonged.

"Trey, baby, take your sister upstairs to the playroom. I got you guys a new movie. Ask Mommy to put it on for you. You can have cookies if you keep quiet." I kissed the side of Lataya's chubby neck, and she smiled at me through her long, baby-doll lashes and giggled. She didn't care what was going on; she'd heard the word "cookies" and was ready to go. Trey groaned and huffed, reluctantly taking her hand and leading her upstairs. It amazed me that Larissa and I could call each other Mommy and the kids just assumed if one said it in regard to doing something it automatically meant go ask the other one.

I glanced down at my watch; it was a little after one in the afternoon. I perched in the large bay window in the living room and saw the blue Mustang pull up to one of the houses down the street. Damn, this shit was making me paranoid. I needed to relax with a capital R. I shouted up toward the kids' playroom, "Ris, watch the kids. I'll be in the pool."

"A'ight, bae."

I walked out to the back of the house and let my sundress slide down my body. The first time I did that shit Ris had a flat-out fit, telling me, "Only white folk go out an' swim in they pool butt-ass naked. Yo' ass end up wit' some kinda bacterial infection, ount wanna hear it." Stripping out of my bra and panties, I laughed at the memory. Our backyard was perfect. Tall white privacy fences ran along both sides of the beach so no one could trespass, and we didn't have to be bothered with the year-round issue of vacationers or beachgoers parking and camping out all over the beach. That was the beauty of the neighborhood: all of the houses were spaced out and they all faced the ocean, so there was no need to worry about nosey-ass neighbors either.

I let the warmth from the sun embrace my bare skin only for a moment before diving into the lukewarm water. I swam a few laps as part of my usual workout routine to keep myself toned, but I didn't want to wear myself out, so I just drifted on my back with my eyes closed for a little while. I sighed; this shit did not help at all. The stress and anxiety was still there. I was wiping water from my eyes when I saw it. It was the briefest movement in the ocean directly in front of me that caught my eye, causing me to freeze mid-motion. The sun glimmered off the water everywhere except for in this one spot. An object bobbed, it was slightly rounded like . . . like a head. I squinted harder and could barely make out a neck and shoulders. And then nothing. It just bobbed under right at the very second that my eyes decided to clearly focus in on it.

I waited, frozen in place, afraid to look anywhere other than where I saw *him,* or it, go under. It didn't resurface. *Okay, woman. You are definitely getting paranoid and super trippin'. It was probably just a dolphin or a sea lion, manatee—fuck. That nigga would not swim five miles out and seven or eight miles across just to stare at the damn house. Or would he?* Not to mention the fact that I still hadn't figured out how anyone from my past had actually found me, or even alerted him to our whereabouts. I must've stayed there staring intently at that square of ocean for a good fifteen to twenty minutes. When nothing resurfaced I gave up and trod back inside, looking over my shoulder every few steps just in case. I made sure to lock all the windows and doors downstairs just in case.

By the time I'd showered and fed the kids it was time to get ready. I was nervous. I wasn't sure what I'd seen out there in the water, but combined with the note that Ris had found, the last thing I wanted to do was leave the house, leave my kids. I pulled the dress Ris picked out over my head and attempted to pull myself together.

"Larissa, what the hell is this ho-ish-lookin', prostitute-in-training shit you got me wearin'?" I stared at myself in the full-length mirror like the woman looking back was a complete stranger.

"Baby, calm da fuck down. Nobody gonna have on nothin' we got on tonight. You look fuckin' hot, too. Like on some straight-up diva shit."

I gawked at myself. The dress was from some collection I'd never heard of and cost entirely too damn much. It was orange, and not no dull spring orange, but bright-ass traffic-cone orange, with black trim around the edges and tiny crystal accents. The neck hung way too low in the front and the back scooped in a V damn near to my ass crack so there was no way I could get away with a bra. It fit tight in all the right places and flared at the arms. It wasn't an ugly dress; it just wasn't me. I always said Ris could not pick out my clothes, but I was such a mess after what I'd seen earlier, I didn't even care. I was dressed. *Fuck it.*

CHAPTER 5

GOOD FOR THE GOOSE—
GOOD FOR THE GANDER

Sitting on the cool leather of the living room couch I impatiently tapped my foot. I was all kinds of nervous about the night ahead. The kids were upstairs with Darla the babysitter and my mind was preoccupied with thoughts of Rasheed. Where the hell was this nigga, and what the hell did he want? How long was he gonna torture us before he showed his ass and started making demands and shit? I'd tried to call the prison to see if he was there and the clerk placed me on hold so long I had to hang up. This happened at least three times.

Scared and frustrated, I'd looked up a few numbers for security services to call, but it was too late in the evening when I'd remembered to do it. I made a mental note to try again one day during the week. Just then the car pulled up to the front of the house as planned. Ris squealed and flew from upstairs so fast she was damn near out of breath.

"Ooh it's here, baby. How I look? My hair okay?"

I stared at her in amazement. She was wearing a bright pink Escada blouse that dipped low in between her breasts, the color complementing her red complexion perfectly. I stared down into her glowing green eyes; I could tell it was definitely more than the makeup and smoky eye shadow lighting up her face.

"You look beautiful, baby, and damn if the club ain't the last place I'm tryin'a go right now."

She giggled and blushed hard. "We'll have time for dat after. Lemme get a li'l nice first and I'll show you a trick when we get back home."

"A trick? What kinda trick you got that I ain't already seen, woman?"

She leaned in and gave me a long kiss before we headed out the door. For the first time in a long time I felt my chest fill up with pride, because I couldn't lie—my wife was bad. She'd somehow managed to pile all her ass into what I'd call about four inches of black fabric and what she had the nerve to be trying to call a damn skirt. Lord, we was gonna get into some fights tonight.

The ride to the club wasn't as long as I thought it would be. Ris made good use of the fully stocked bar· and was a lot more than nice by the time we finished the forty-five-minute drive into Miami. As our limo pulled up to the front of the club I texted Keyshawn to let him know we were outside. I was surprised when Yylannia came out to the car.

"Well hello, *mi* gorgeous ladies. Key is inside holding the table, ordering foods. Come—come." She waved her elegant, li'l skinny hand and started to cat-walk away. She was wearing a short, tight black dress that fit her like a second skin. Her jet-black hair hung down her back in long layers that almost touched her ass. I was in awe. She looked exotic and classy.

"Oh my God. That's her, Chelle. She's beautiful and soooo damn skinny. Um, did her ass jus' say 'foods'?"

Yylannia did have a strange accent and way of saying things sometimes. It wasn't Spanish or French, more of a mixture of the two. Hell I'd just settle for calling it a "Franish"-ass accent. Ris's tipsy ass giggled and mock cat-walked behind her. We completely by-passed the line to get inside. It was wrapped damn near completely around the entire complex but we just followed Ms. Walk Like a Model Everywhere and the bouncers nodded and let us inside. I could literally feel bitches glaring and hatin' on us and I actually enjoyed it for once, mentally reminding myself not to trip or do anything embarrassing trying to be cute in front of all these damn onlookers.

The club was packed with men and women, white, black. Mostly white. Mostly women—let me rephrase—mostly model, gold-digger, video, actress, and party-girl types. On this particular night they were playing house music, and I already knew Ris was gonna have an attitude if we didn't get her semi fucked up before she realized they weren't playing any hip-hop. We walked toward a private entryway with so much security you would have thought President Obama himself was up in there. Yylannia just breezed us past and it was like we'd walked into an entirely different club.

The ambiance was sexier, way more elegant than the estrogen zoo we'd just passed through. The entire floor was made of white glass, and changed colors, going from purple to neon pink to blue. Smoke machines filled the entire area in a cool white mist; I reached out and grabbed Ris's hand to make sure we didn't lose her. She was quiet, which was a good thing; it meant she was in awe. We swept past booth after booth. The entire area was about the size of a large restaurant and all of it was exclusively for members-only VIP. You had to pay a yearly fee just to be able to reserve a booth on any given Friday or Saturday, and that was only if they had availability and even then you still had to run up a tab in the thousands in order to keep your spot. All of the booths had round white leather sofas or chaises longues and tables, and the outsides were covered with white curtains that could remain open or be completely closed for privacy.

We arrived at a booth toward the back where Key was sitting with two other extremely beautiful women. He looked completely edible in a deep grey Gucci button down and dark grey slacks. Yylannia scooted in beside him and patted the seat next to her, directing me to sit down.

"Hello, everyone, this is Larissa, my wife." I didn't want to hesitate in making the introductions lest Ris take offense and start to think something was up, as she was accustomed to doing.

"Don't be so formal. Just call me Lania and him Key, over beside Key you have Chanel and Keisha." Lania smiled, beaming straight, blindingly perfect white teeth and deep dimples that I hadn't noticed before. I nodded to the two women who were paying Ris and me no mind. Chanel was a gorgeous woman the same dark chocolate tone as Keyshawn, with large, dark, expressive eyes that reminded me of one of those Japanime characters. She'd completely dismissed Ris and me and was whispering something in Key's ear, causing him to chuckle and whisper back. I felt a small twinge of jealousy at their obvious closeness; guessed the joke was on me for thinking his ass wasn't like every other nigga with good looks and money. Why I was letting shit like that bother me I had no idea; it's not like he had a chance with me anyway. I looked away quickly, scared my expression might give away my thoughts, and Keisha, to my surprise, was actually watching me watch them. She smiled at me smugly before kissing Chanel on the neck, glancing at me from the corner of her eye. *Bitch, I was not checking out yo' girl,* I thought.

"Um, Lania, you are soooo beautiful. I'm sorry, I'm just a li'l tipsy. There was free liquor on—I mean in—our limo. And oooh, Keyshawn. I mean Key. If I get me a basketball would you sign it?"

All I could do was look down in horror and roll my eyes, and no, the damn liquor in the limo was not *free;* every drop she chugalugged was comin' out of my pocket. I sighed a long, loud sigh.

"Yeah, I'd be more than happy to, ma. Jus' give it to Michelle over there and it's a done deal. So, how about we start off with a bottle of rosé and some mutha-fuckin' shots, 'cause I don't know about y'all but my ass is thirsty."

I smiled apologetically at Keyshawn, thankful for the icebreaker.

I wasn't sure how many glasses of champagne or how many shots we were in, but things were definitely starting to get fun. We'd each taken turns talking about strange and random sex facts. Thanks to Lania, I now knew that some female penguins actually engaged in prostitution to get pebbles from "single" guy pen-guins to build their nests. She kept looking at Chanel the whole time she was telling the story, which had me weak as hell. If I didn't know better I'd have said Chanel was giving Key a hand job under the table; he'd suddenly gotten extremely quiet and they both seemed overly interested in something down there.

There was a bunch of commotion at the entrance, drawing everyone's attention. Two bouncers came in and ordered the people in the booth behind us to leave. I could hear the guy complaining and asking for a man-ager.

"Damn, what's going on?" I asked, glancing around cautiously. *After everything I've put myself through to plan this shit out, they'd better not ask us to move or my ass is going to raise pure hell.* In the center of the bodyguards there was a smaller guy with piercing crystal-grey eyes carrying a Louis Vuitton briefcase, and a group of women flocked around him. I almost twisted my neck trying to get a better look at who he was.

"Who is he supposed to be?" I had to ask when I couldn't figure it out. He didn't look like anyone I'd seen anywhere before.

"That's Angelo Testa, consider him like a billionaire." Lania waved at him and smiled. Keyshawn nodded in the little man's direction. A few of the girls with him looked familiar. I assumed they were models or actresses. One in particular stayed plastered to his side. She was shorter than the others, thick and light skinned. I couldn't make her face out completely but I thought it was the girl from "Pon de Replay"? Maybe. Every video I'd ever seen ran through my head but I only got to see her for a split second before the curtains were drawn and they were having their own private party, in there doing Lord knows what. Ris was zoned out so I couldn't ask her where the hell I'd seen the girl before. Eight different security guys stood guard outside around the booth and I must admit I was impressed. Lania suggested we all get up and dance, but I realized I needed to pee so bad I couldn't sit still anymore.

"Lania, hold on, where's the restroom?"

"I'll take you; it's hard to explain and I have to go too."

Ris looked like she was on the verge of passing out at the table. She either said she did or didn't have to pee, I couldn't tell. But she didn't get up so I guessed it wasn't a yes. It'd been awhile since we'd drunk together and I was gonna have so much fun reminding her in the morning that she'd lost her touch. There would definitely be no tricks tonight; she was in no position to show me anything.

Chanel and Keisha said they'd wait for us at the table. I followed Lania through a maze of booths and a blur of familiar faces I'd seen on TV. She waved and made small talk and I tapped her on her shoulder, reminding her that this was urgent.

The bathroom was just as luxurious as the VIP area. The lighting was dimmed and the speakers in the ceiling played the club music overhead. There was an actual sitting area with small palm fronds and soft chaises longues. There was even an actual walk-in toilet like you would use in someone's house, not a stall like you'd expect to find. I handled my business and walked out, washing my hands and straightening my dress. I looked toward the chaise longue where I'd left Lania and didn't see her. I had just barely opened my mouth to call out and ask her where she'd disappeared to before her lips were on mine. She wore J'adore Dior perfume and she tasted like rosé and fresh cherries and yes—I noticed all of that before I broke myself out of the spell I was in. Pulling my lips from hers I began shaking my head no. I was in such a complete shock, I couldn't make a sound.

I hadn't realized how beautiful she actually was, completely dismissing my initial judgment of her at the house when I'd first seen her. Her eyes were a light golden brown and in the dim lighting it looked like they were aglow from the inside. Like the reflection you see from a flame in the glass when you burn a candle in a hurricane jar. We had a complete conversation without saying a single word, her eyes boldly telling me, "I want you." I backed up a step, shaking my head again, silently saying, "I'm married—this cannot go down." Biting her lower lip, eyebrow raised, she narrowed her slanted golden cat eyes, soundlessly telling me, "I get what I want—and I want you now." My eyes widened in an utter look of "Oh shit." *I'm such a punk*. I mentally slapped myself for this one, because she had me.

I wasn't used to being challenged or pursued by a woman, not since Ris, and it caught me off guard when she came at me again. *I shouldn't have had so many tequila shots. The liquor is definitely my damn alibi and I'm sticking to it.* My eyes closed in anticipation. I was completely ready for the sensual assault of Dior and cherry rosé to consume me—and it did. My hands had a mind of their own and I let them roam freely until I felt warm, smooth, baby-soft skin.

I slid my hand upward, raising her dress as I went. I gently caressed her left breast in one hand, lightly teasing her nipple until she moaned and playfully bit the corner of my lip. The sound she made was low, sultry—every hair on the back of my neck stood on edge. I explored with my other hand, allowing it to slide down the soft, muscled outline of her stomach to the soft lift of her ass. My eyes opened and I gasped in shocked surprise when I stroked her hairless wonder, amazed at how smooth, soft, and *wet* she was. *Shit.*

Mental note number 543: get a damn Brazilian wax. No matter how much they say that shit hurts it's damn sure worth it. To be so thin and frail looking, Lania was *strong*. She had somehow backed me up against the sink and had lifted me up onto it in one solid movement. She roughly wrapped one of her hands around my neck, gently choking me while lightly digging her nails into my skin at the same time. I couldn't take it; it had to be the sweetest torture I'd ever felt. Ris didn't have nails because she'd bite them off, but damn she needed to grow or buy some.

Lania took complete control over everything: my body and my senses. I could feel her fingers burning a trail of heat up my inner thigh and her mouth left mine to take advantage of the deep, plunging neckline in the front of my dress and the fact that I wasn't wearin' a bra. The pressure building in between my thighs was so much it was becoming damn near painful. She was slowly sliding my panties to one side, teasing me at first, letting her finger trail ever so softly across my already throbbing lips. I was about to be extremely embarrassed because I was entirely too damn wet to just be on some second base–type shit, but I couldn't help it. She shoved two fingers deep inside me and I swear I almost exploded right there on the spot.

"Michelle?"

In my tequila-sex haze I almost responded until I realized it wasn't Lania saying my name. Someone pounded frantically on the bathroom door.

"Michelle? Are you in there? I think I'm gonna be sick." Larissa was knocking on the bathroom door.

"Shit." We both cursed quietly. It was like I was doused with cold water and simultaneously hit over the head. Frustration and disappointment in myself set in all at once. I hopped off the sink and straightened my dress and panties, checking my hair in the mirror. Lania arranged her dress and recomposed herself before walking back over to the chaise longue, looking as if she'd been there all along. I unlocked the door and Ris rushed in, eyeing us both suspiciously.

"What the fuck took you so long? The fuck, Michelle?" She was wobbling back and forth.

I raised my hands as if waiving the white flag. "Larissa, not here—not now. Nothin' was goin' on, baby, calm down."

She pointed over in Lania's direction, staggering toward her. "You bitch, I seen you, prissy, Frenchy bitch—lookin' at my bitch."

Lord, I must have turned five shades of red I was so damn embarrassed. I grabbed Ris by her shoulders and turned her to face me so I could at least lie to her directly in the eyes. "Ris, baby, I promise nothing . . ." Shit, before the words could leave my mouth Larissa did some kinda behind-the-back drunk crossover, goin' around me like fuckin' Jordan back in '93 and was on Lania's ass before I could blink.

"Michelle, get your bitch before I kill her."

Ris went flyin' back across the room, and I just stood there, eyes wide as fuck, staring in stunned silence. I told y'all that skinny heffa was *strong*. She'd pushed Larissa's ass up off of her so damn hard I was in shock.

"Ugh, Chelle, I'm gonna be sick." Larissa was definitely done as she staggered toward the stall in the corner.

I followed her into the bathroom and held her hair back just as she let go. "Damn, Ris, I think you're ready to go, baby." She surprised me by shaking her head no in between frame-racking heaves. I looked over at Lania, who surprised me even further by just shruggin' as if this was a normal thing for her ass.

"Well, Risi-cup, I think it's safe to say you definitely can't handle your liquor anymore. Let's go get yo' ass some water so you can sober the fuck up."

"The hell I can't. I's jus' makin' room fa' more." She chuckled, and I helped her fix her hair and walked her back out to the table. Keyshawn was right where we left him, looking just as handsome with his two concubines, waiting patiently as ever.

"Y'all good?" Keyshawn asked, barely glancing in my direction.

Lania slid back into her place beside him and gave him an awkward smile. They exchanged a look, or I thought they exchanged a look; it was so brief I could have possibly imagined it. I just didn't want to seem like I was imposing, and I definitely didn't want to be labeled as the woman with the wife who gets drunk and acts a complete mess in public.

"So, my mans is comin' to hang out with us if y'all up for it."

Ris flopped down into the booth and answered before I could even open up my mouth and come up with an excuse to get us out of there.

"Our asses is up for it. Is he anotha basketball player? Who is it?" She was pouring herself another glass of champagne, but more of it was ending up on the table than in her champagne flute.

"He's the owner of the team. Cool dude. Here, let me pour that for you, you are my guest." He directed his gaze toward me after filling her glass less than full. "Very good connect to have. You never know when you need to know someone like him."

With that statement the business part of me kicked in and I sat my ass down. "Key, pour me a glass too, please." *Never know when you'll need to know an NBA team owner, especially in the housing industry. That's some super official shit right there.*

It didn't take long for Curtis Daniels to arrive; he was a tall, older man with greying hair at the temples on either side of his head. I can't lie; he looked like money.

Keyshawn got up to greet him when he came over, and introduced him. It was a damn near buzz kill having him at the table and I was honestly happy for it. Key's playful demeanor immediately went out the window and he was acting like a perfect gentleman. If I weren't mistaken I'd say he was actually uncomfortable, but I guessed I would be a bit out of my element too if my boss wanted to come hang out at a damn club when I was tryin' to let loose and drink.

"Excuse me. Sir Angelo extends his graciousness." A waiter had appeared at our booth with a bottle of Château Lafite Rothschild Pauillac. My eyes widened and we all looked back toward the booth, but the curtains were still drawn.

"Send it back. I've already paid for champagne." Keyshawn surprised even me, but Lania said what we were all thinking.

"Key, that's a three thousand dollar bottle of champagne. This isn't a dick-measuring contest; are you trying to offend him on purpose?"

Keyshawn acted like he didn't even hear her.

"Tell Angelo we send our appreciation. Keyshawn, that pride will make you lose more than it will ever earn you if you don't get it under control." Curtis accepted a glass from the waiter and I couldn't help but wonder what Key had against that Angelo guy.

Curtis's sophisticated demeanor was a good balance to the group. It kept Ris from suicide tag-teaming shots and glasses of champagne left and right, giving her a little time to sober up. Once the guys got on the subject of basketball plays and seasons and playoffs, I decided it was a good time to call it a night, and I pulled a reluctant somebody away from the table and out to the limo so we could go home.

Ris pouted the first half of the ride and slept the rest of the way. My phone rang. I didn't recognize the number but figured it must be Keyshawn; I even got excited and dared it to be Curtis.

"Hello?"

"Enjoy your time while you still can, bitch." That's all that was said and the call disconnected. The voice sounded like something out of a horror movie. I knew there were plenty of apps on iPhones and other programs that could mask your voice, make it raspy or deeper, but why would Rasheed want to go through all the trouble? Was scaring me that serious? I dialed the number back and it went to a Google voice service that said the call couldn't be completed. My heart felt like it was doing clumsy flips in my chest. Someone needed to put a stop to this shit. The phone vibrated again, showing yet another number I didn't recognize. I hit answer and didn't say a word. I slid the phone to my ear, my heart beating in my throat, afraid to hear whatever murder, death, kill threat I would get next but ready to cuss someone the fuck out.

"Umm, hello? Michelle?"

A woman? It took me a second to place her voice. "Lania? Hey, I'm sorry I . . . I had the phone on mute." I wasn't in the mood for her cat-and-mouse bullshit right this second, especially not with Ris asleep right here, liable to wake up and ask a million questions.

"So, I honestly don't do this that often and I am in understanding with your situation, but I'd really like to be seeing you again. Soon if that is possible."

I had to shake my head yet again at her "Frannish" but that low, sultry voice of hers, it was like warm spiced caramel, and I had an instantaneous flashback of what it sounded like when she . . .

I popped that thought bubble before it could float any higher. I had too much going on to entertain this type of bullshit right now. Ris adjusted her head on my shoulder in her sleep and I stiffened.

"Lania, I can't. I'm sorry about what happened tonight too, but I just can't. I've gotta go okay?" I didn't even wait for her to respond. Suddenly I realized that I'd just hung up on one of *Maxim*'s top one hundred.

Actually I think she was numbered as the twenty-eighth most beautiful woman in the world. I exhaled loudly. My neck was starting to hurt. I needed to be as rational and real about this situation as possible and with the way things were going, Rasheed was probably going to try to kill me. The key word was try, because there was no way I was giving up my life without a damn good fight. That muthafucka had another thing coming if he thought otherwise.

CHAPTER 6

WHAT'S MINE IS YOURS AND
WHAT'S YOURS IS STILL YOURS

Boy oh boy. I almost went slam the fuck off and gave away the fact that my ass wasn't for real drunk sleeping on Michelle's shoulder. I'd adjusted my head so I could hear her conversation better. The first one was quick and weird. I couldn't really hear it that well but based on the way she tensed up it wasn't good news. But the second one, *whew,* I almost nodded my head right into her lap because I was straining so hard to hear. I just *knew* something was up with that pretty-ass model Frenchy bitch mispronouncing- shit-for-no-damn-reason streetwalking ho. *Oh, I bet Chelle ain't even know all that shit.* Keyshawn was on his phone and Keisha had started talkin' all low to Chanel when they left sayin' some shit 'bout Lania needin' her to escort some nigga somewhere so they needed to ditch our party. An' here I was kissin' her ass thinkin' she on some top model shit and she over here running hoes.

Lania's ass had just hopped up too quick to help out when Michelle needed to go piss at the club. An' when Chanel and Keisha had the nerve to ask if I was okay with them going together, it took everything in my power to keep me at the table for as long as I sat there. It took a helluva lot more for me to embarrass myself and stick my damn finger down my throat when Chelle wasn't paying attention so I could throw up. My ass wasn't gonna be sick. I just needed an excuse to whoop that bitch's ass, and being drunk just seemed like a good enough'a one to me, shit.

My Spidey-muthafuckin'-sense was already on ten; I ain't need Tweedledee and Tweedledum-ass pointin' shit out like my ass stupid. I didn't know if Michelle did or didn't do anything up in that damn bathroom, but just in case, I got my ass whoopin' in just for her or that bitch even thinkin' 'bout doin' that shit. Point blank, that's all the fuck it took. Little Ms. Lania's ass was on my muthafuckin' radar. Period.

I could feel the limo roll to a stop. Michelle kissed me on my forehead and I blinked a few times, trying to adjust my eyes since they'd been closed the entire ride.

"Hey, you lush, we're home." She gave me one of her fake-ass "I'm trying to act like nothing's wrong" smiles. It was damn obvious she was worried about something. I just hoped she wasn't thinking about that bitch.

"Is somethin' wrong, bae?" I acted like I was still a little hazy from all the liquor, but I was super alert, watching everything.

"Nothin' baby. I'm jus' tired, it's close to four in the morning."

We climbed out of the car and made our way up to the darkened house, both of us trying to look normal as fuck while secretly eyeballing every tree, shadow, and bush. Most of the main lights were off in the house but the sitter had left the foyer lit. She was sitting in the living room, doing some shit with these long-ass needles. *I guess that's what the fuck knitting looks like. Boring,* I thought. Darla was an older, maybe late-forties white lady with stringy brown hair. Michelle found her through some kind of nanny referral service. She came with this long list of celebrity clients, a resume, a background check, all that shit. The needles clinked together as she dropped them into her little nanny knapsack and walked over to us.

"Hello, misses." She always called us that like we weren't some damn grown-ass women, always talkin' in her polite little field mouse voice. I bet she had a gazillion cats at home an' shit, or a million of those little white china baby dolls and she be talkin' to 'em and shit like they real kids. That's what the fuck she looked like in her pink and white "Nannies 'R' Us" uniform that the agency made her wear.

"A visitor came by not long after you left. As instructed I did not approach nor open the door. The children are upstairs in bed. They are very well behaved and beautiful little ones. Feel free to reserve my services anytime."

I didn't hear a damn thing after the word "visitor." *Who in the hell came by the house?*

You would've thought the two of us were wanted fugitives the way we suddenly looked at each other. Both of us asked the same question in our heads without needing to speak it out loud in front of this person who didn't need to know our business.

"Darla, I'll see you out. Thank you so, so much for your time this evening." Michelle took over and walked Darla toward the front door. She locked and bolted the double front doors, set the alarm, and together we went down the hall into the study that we never used. It wasn't a large study, I guessed. I ain't never had a house with a study so I wouldn't know. Michelle picked all the books that lined all the walls, most of which she'd said she read. I'd skimmed through a few but they were all, "think about this, grow rich that," a ton of shit I couldn't get into. The only one that I'd actually read was an old voodoo tale that scared the hell out my ass and I ain't touched another one since.

Our entire house minus Chelle's "sanctuary" had hardwood flooring, which I personally hated. Michelle's reasoning was it would not only add value to the house but it'd be easier to keep clean with the kids. When I told her I didn't like hardwood floors because they're cold, *Bam,* she had them install heaters *in the floors*. Nothing, not a single thing, in the house was mine or had my touch. Everything was Michelle's vision or Michelle's idea or customized to Michelle's liking or her idea of comfort. She'd furnished and picked it all out before we moved from Virginia as a "gift." She ain't even bother to think that I'd have liked to at least have some say in what color walls I'd want to stare at every damn day, or what kind of couch I'd want my ass on? Hell, I ain't even like the colors or the design on the sheets on the damn bed. *Ugh.*

We walked up to the oversized mahogany desk in the center. Michelle plopped down in the leather seat in front of the touchscreen HP and I sat in her lap, since it was the only place to sit.

"You ever even learn how to use that damn camera system?" I was being a smartass on purpose. Since the day it was installed I'd never figured out how to use it and I sure as hell wasn't sure if she had.

"The man said it's twenty-four hours and backed up to a main server, all we have to do is enter the password and we can view the footage."

I wasn't sure why I never thought of it before. The cameras were all some state-of-the-art bullshit, teeny as hell and hidden around the outside of the house. We had one at the front door, one overlooking the garage, and I was pretty sure there was another that looked out over the back toward the pool.

"So why don't you just use the li'l touchscreen pad things that's all over the house?"

We had one in every damn room. They looked like mini TVs on the wall beside the light switches and they controlled damn near everything. You could dim the lights, turn the music on or off in each room, and, *duh,* look outside using the cameras.

"Because, Ris, those cameras are real time, we need to access shit that's already passed. So we need to go back a few hours. After a week the files are archived so we can't access them." She sounded irritated. There was no reason for her to talk to me in such a know-it-all tone.

"Well damn you ain't gotta snap at my ass. I was jus' askin'." *Shit, I'll keep my suggestions to myself.* She sure did know a lot about all of this, and my ass just felt more and more alienated as she put in her password and pulled up her site, more shit I was oblivious to. It was a wonder she didn't spy on me when I was home with the kids.

She scrolled her finger along the screen and the footage zoomed forward through the day, and I watched us leave in the limo, and a few minutes later a white flower delivery van pulled up, and we watched as a figure got out and walked up to the house with what had to be the largest bouquet of lilies in history. The sun was setting and it was shadowy, so we honestly couldn't tell if it was a man or a woman. *Damn, why hadn't Darla turned on the front light?* We might have been able to see something if she had. He or she had on a huge gardening hat and the lilies completely blocked the side view of their face so watching the video any further was pointless. Michelle groaned and touched stop on the screen.

"What? It's just a damn florist. Probably from one of your fuckin' side hoes." Jealousy seared through me in an instant, flashed with a mixture of anger and pain. It wasn't anyone sendin' me flowers, that was for damn sure. Climbing off her lap I started to make my way upstairs, intent on thinking my way out of this no-win situation with her lying ass. The thought of being close to her and thinking that once again Rasheed or Lania or whoever the fuck else was touching her or sharing her with me was tearing me up inside.

"Larissa. It doesn't bother you that this florist had on a sun hat and was trying to deliver flowers damn near in the middle of the night? Every house out here has security cameras somewhere. You don't think whoever it was wasn't trying to hide their face on purpose?"

Her words fell on deaf ears. She was pleading her case, trying to cover up her lover's tracks because the flowers probably should've gone to her fuckin' office and not to our damn house.

"And they just happened to know you love lilies. Most deliveries for most normal companies do stop at nine, Michelle." I couldn't hide the smirk on my face. Oooh my ass was heated. I stormed out to the garage, intent on rolling me a fat one and putting some clouds up in the air because this bitch done straight chased away all of the buzz I had. She had some nerve having niggas sending flowers and shit up here, and then on top of that Lania's ass trying to get at her with me right there just feet away.

I stomped into the garage, the humidity immediately making me break out into a sweat, pissing me off even further. I looked at the layer of dust gathering on my silver Jag and my candy-red Mercedes coupe, both gifts from Michelle. I needed my own got-damn car that I paid for. Not something that was given to me like I was a spoiled brat or someone's child who needed an allowance and permission to do things. At one point in time I thought this was the life I wanted. To have someone just take care of me and just give. She gave me clothes, gave me money. Michelle gave me everything I had. I realized now that the problem with someone doing all the damn giving is that at any moment they could take it all back. I needed to do something, and I needed to do it fast. If our marriage wasn't legal in Florida and she wanted me gone or if I decided I wanted to leave.

The thought of me putting up with so much and walking away with absolutely nothing made my stomach twist into knots. The main reason Michelle even had the nerve to have half of what she had was because of me and did she ever truly show me any appreciation? *Fuck no.* I helped pull her up from her knees and now she wanted to just walk away. We only had one solid rule between the two of us and to this day as far as I knew neither of us had ever broken it. We'd both sworn to never lock our phones and to respect each other's privacy by not going through each other's shit. Pacing in the garage, I couldn't help feeling like a caged animal. Like one of those damn dwarf leopards I'd seen in Trey's zoo magazines. Yup, my ass was a damn endangered ocelot and my habitat, my cubs, and everything else was on the verge of being wiped out if I didn't start fighting. My lifestyle, my way of living, was in jeopardy and so was Lataya's. My mind was made up.

CHAPTER 7

FRENEMIES

I waited until Michelle's ass was at work before I called her, and I prayed that this bitch would actually be cool and not turn around and tell Michelle about our conversation.

"Larissa? Who? Oh, oh I remember your ass. Little Jackie Chan." She sounded like her ass was half asleep when she'd answered the phone.

"Oh yeah, 'bout that. I'm so sorry I was hammered. I hope you can forgive me."

"It is fine. We've all been there. No harm, no foul. What is it you're wanting?" She yawned loud as hell in my ear. *Well, damn, she sure isn't the sugar-coatin' type.*

"So um, Lania, I heard you be on some shit, an' I need to earn some extra money. Fast." I hadn't slept one bit all damn night thinking about what I would say, and was nervous as fuck about finally callin' her, but decided to go ahead an' go through with it.

"And what exactly is this you think you have heard?"

Well, shit, here goes nothin', I thought. Either I'd heard wrong or I'd heard right.

"I want to be an escort, no sex though. Just go on a few dates, look pretty or whatever, an' then bring my ass home. That's it. I heard you could set that up." I held my breath.

"Ahhh. I see, and what does your wife say about this?"

"She don't know and ain't never gonna know."

"Okay. As far as you know I am the alpha, I am the queen of this shit. You want to run with the wolves—you must earn your place in the pack. You're new so no, you won't get first pick or top choice. You have to work your way up."

"So what does that mean, what do I need to do?"

"You won't make as much, the girls who make the most do . . . how should I say . . . . um, favors, but you aren't bad looking so I can work with you. Fix yourself up, text me a picture, full body. I have a client who needs a girl for an event tonight at ten. If you are up to standard, a car will pick you up and drop you off when it's over. One of my men will follow you all evening."

"So when you say 'special favors,' you mean what?" My hands were gettin' sweaty at the excitement an' possibility of doing something new, dangerous.

"I mean, I pay you to go on a date, they'll offer you extra for *extra shit*. I warn you now, sometimes clients can get a bit testy, especially if they drink or do too much drugs. Don't drink or do anything with them so you don't make any kind of decisions you'll regret. You earn three thou, my cut a thousand of that."

Damn. Three grand to sit and look cute. Fuck yes. "Abso-fuckin-lutely. I'll send you a pic in a minute. Thank you, Lania."

I rushed off the phone to get myself sexified. I threw on a red lacy corset that tied up the sides. I glued on some dramatic strip lashes and brushed on a little light makeup. I stood around in the bathroom and played around with the camera on my phone until I had a few pictures I was happy with. I sent them to Lania and waited anxiously for her to let me know if my ass was gonna be able to escort.

Very very nice. Be ready at 9:15 send me your address. btw dress for a play.

That was the text I got back not more than ten minutes later. *Damn, what the fuck do I have that I can wear to a play, and how the fuck am I gonna get around Michelle?* The answer came to me when I was taking my shower.

Michelle got home at her usual time and I ain't feel like wearing a damn thing she'd bought me. Until I'd earned some money and bought myself some of my own shit, I'd prefer to just fuckin' walk around naked. *Fuck it.*

I crushed up some valiums that were left over from the time she hurt her back rearranging the living room furniture. Them things always knocked her slam the fuck out. Whenever she got home from work she'd usually go straight to the fridge and get a glass of tea. That was her routine. Well, I'd dumped all the tea outta the pitcher except for like half a glass, and mixed in the crushed pills, adding some extra sugar so it wouldn't taste bitter.

"You been home all day, drank all the damn tea, and didn't think to make any more, Larissa?" were the first words she said when she got home from work. I just looked at her ass and raised my eyebrow.

"So you're still doing that no-talking shit I see. Okay. Okay. Well, I'm not making any more. Y'all can all drink water tomorrow for all I care. "

I watched her ass pour that last little bit of tea into a glass, thinking, *yup, drink up, drink up, sweetie.* Gigglin' to myself, I just carried my ass on upstairs to start getting ready for my night.

***

I waited out front, smoking some of the shit Shanice had sent me to help calm my nerves. At nine-fifteen two black Lincoln Town Cars pulled up into our driveway and Michelle was on the couch, unconscious, just like I knew she'd be. I tiptoed out the front door, wearing one of her wack-ass black skirts and a red button-down Michael Kors top. I couldn't resist throwing on a pair of matching red pumps; conservative was not a word in my vocabulary. I was going to be escorting Darnell Wiggs Jr. to see *Le . . . Miser . . . Misera . . .* Fuck, I couldn't pronounce that shit. It was some kinda French play. All I knew was I didn't know this actor and I didn't know the damn play and they both sounded boring as hell. The three Gs I'd get at the end of the night was the only thing exciting me about the whole damn evening.

When we pulled up in front of the theatre my ass was immediately turned off by all the old, rigid, stuffy-collared folk in suits and ties walking toward the place. Darnell walked up to my car and my frowned disappeared. It was time for my escort acting to begin. He wasn't a bad-looking older man; you know, dudes ain't my thing to begin with any damn way, but he was all right, I guess. He looked around forty-five, brown skin, he was kinda pudgy looking with droopy eyes.

"Well hello to you, gorgeous. I'ma have to tell Ms. Lania she done sent me a million-dolla one this time." He grabbed my hand and helped me out of the car. I smiled, not sure what to say back since I ain't never did this shit before. He extended his arm, and after glancing around nervously I'd seen that some of the other women had their hands on the inside of the guys' arms, so I placed my hand on the inside of his.

"How are you doin', honey?"

I almost tripped over my own damn feet and fell on my face. Out of all the pet name, he couldn't have called me sweetie or baby? I smiled at him weakly, trying to push all thoughts of Rasheed and Michelle's drama out of my head.

"I'm good. Thanks."

We walked into the darkened theatre and up to the top. He'd gotten us these special box seats; I guessed they were more expensive, I didn't know. If I was gonna watch a play or anything I'd rather be in the front row than in a seat far up and off to the side, but hey—these rich folk be having they own warped opinions on luxury. I think they just like sitting over top of muthafuckas personally.

I was half asleep halfway through the play when Darnell leaned over, his breath smelling like he'd gone in on a plate of chitlins with extra shit, all up against the side of my face. I did my best not to turn away completely.

"Baby, you play wit' it an' I'll give you another three grand."

Cringing, I tried to hear the words over the stank comin' out of his mouth. *Play with what?* was the first thought that echoed in my brain, but I already knew what the hell he meant. Lania said the girls who sucked, fucked, and did extras made the extra money, but my ass had never even seen a real dick let alone touched one. I shook my head no and watched the stage, silently kissing the thought of $6,000 good-bye.

Once again, "Yuck-Mouf" was assaultin' the side of my face, whispering loud as hell, about to melt the fake eyelashes off of my damn eyelids.

"C'mon, can't nobody see up here; it's dark."

I heard the zipper of his pants slide down. "Gimme yo' hand, baby. It's three thousand more. Easy money. Make Daddy D happy, baby."

Maybe it's because my ass was high and I just wanted this muthafucka to stop whisperin' air shit all upside my damn head. I closed my eyes and let him take my hand. I was trying to tell myself it was just like one of our straps at home. *But nah, our straps ain't got super nappy taco meat hair all around 'em and fat rolls.* It was like trying to grab a hold of a short-ass soggy eggroll. Darnell kept his hand over mind, directin' it up and down until his li'l eggroll firmed up. I tried to watch the actors and shit on stage and think about what I'd cook for dinner tomorrow—anything but what the fuck was going on with my other hand.

I almost gagged when I felt his mouth brush the side of my neck. He was breathin' vapors of shit fumes right into my damn hair. He started to move my hand faster. I felt like either we was gonna start a forest fire or Indian burn the skin off his dick, and then his body jerked like he was having muscle spasms and charley horses at the same time. Snatching my hand back from beneath his I cringed, trying to find some place to wipe away the slimy, hot mass of yuck that was now sliding down my fingers toward my wrist.

"Honey, you are amazing. Hold on a sec, baby. I got a handkerchief for you." He handed me the small piece of white cloth and I wiped my hand, still feeling like I needed to scour that muthafucka in bleach.

When the play ended Darnell walked me to my car and climbed into the back with me to pay me out for the night. He started to hand me six thousand but when I reached for it he pulled it back.

"Ten if we fuck."

What the hell? If this old raggedy stank-breath nigga ain't give me my damn money . . . His ass was looking like he just knew I was about to say yes, too. "Sorry, Darnell, I don't have sex."

His droopy face scrunched up in anger. "Stuck-up bitch. You gon' regret that shit."

Money flew all around the back seat. He'd thrown all $6,000 at my face and slammed out of the car. Lania's driver looked back at me through the rearview mirror.

"You okay back there? Not too many girls tell Darnell no."

"Guess my ass ain't too many girls huh?"

He smiled and handed me a few of the hundreds that had managed to land up in the front with him, and I texted Lania to let her know everything went well, and she replied fast as hell.

Good I have another one for you tomorrow night if you're up to it?

I stared at the message. She didn't get a cut of any of the money earned from the extra shit I decided to do. So minus her little thousand, I was up $5,000 for just one night's worth of work. Not bad, even though I had to touch that nigga's nasty-ass li'l sausage dick. *What the fuck, might as well get it while I can.*

I'm up—down whateva lol.

We pulled back up at the house late as hell and I crept my ass inside. Michelle was still asleep on the couch where I'd left her ass, so I went upstairs and showered fast as hell and got my ass in bed like I'd been there all along. *Damn, how the hell am I gonna get outta the house two nights in a row . . .*

CHAPTER 8

SPECIAL DELIVERY—SPECIAL K

Michelle went to work as usual and I had all day to plan a way to get ready for my second official day on the job. I didn't know what time Lania would need me so I needed to figure out a way to get up outta the damn house without comin' off kinda suspicious. The damn pill bottle only had two valiums left in it and if there was only one or none left up in there, who was the first person you think she'd look at? My ass. So the valiums were not an option. I texted Lania.

Don't think I can do tonight. Put da wife to sleep and now I'm outta pills.

I stared out the kitchen window at the pool. *Damn shame I ain't never learn how to swim.* That water was lookin' nice as fuck and it was hot as hell outside. My phone beeped.

I'll send Key over with somethin jus put a few drops of it on the brim of her glass or in the bottom—night night I promise.

No more than twenty minutes later the doorbell rang.

"Who's at the door, Mommy? Who's that?" Trey's li'l nosey ass was all in the damn way.

"It's ya damn daddy. Li'l nigga, it ain't for you, now get the hell on upstairs before I beat yo' li'l ass."

I was surprised to see that Keyshawn actually brought me a signed ball.

"You remembered. Damn, thanks." I was already tryin' to figure out how much I could sell that shit on eBay for.

"Cute kid. He look jus' like Michelle."

I looked back. Trey was still at the top of the stairs. I frowned up at his ass, which sent him runnin'. "Whateva. Lania said you was bringin' me somethin." I ain' have time to be dawdlin' with this nigga. We walked into the livin' room and he handed me a little brown bottle.

"It's Special K, strong shit. You don't need a lot; just a couple of drops or she could die okay?"

I nodded. "So what else can y'all get?" My weed stash was damn near gone, and if I was gonna be doin' any more of these jobs, I was gonna need to re-up or somethin' quick.

"We can get anything you want. Just say the word."

Damn, I thought, *now that is what the fuck I'm talkin' about.* Florida wasn't looking so bad after all.

I walked in the house at my usual time and all was quiet, surprisingly. There was no sign of Larissa or the kids. I set my briefcase down and walked into the living room, no toys all over the place, no babies, no wife. This was strange. Kicking off my shoes I made my way into the kitchen, thinking everyone must be in there, but no, it was empty. I was shocked to see a plate sitting in the middle of the counter with a lonely tuna salad sandwich on it and a glass of iced tea beside it. There was no way I was eatin' that shit. Larissa put so much sugar and sweet pickle relish in her tuna and chicken salad it's a wonder she ain't have diabetes by now. I would do that glass of tea though; that's the only thing she made perfect. It was all impressive; maybe this was her way of saying sorry.

Sitting at the counter, I flipped through most of the day's mail and drank my tea, wondering where everyone had wandered off to. I was halfway through with my glass when I thought I heard Lataya laughin' upstairs, and I got up to go see what she was up to. The room swayed and it felt like I had the worst case of vertigo ever. Everything in the kitchen was rocking back and forth, and as hard as I tried I couldn't focus my eyes on anything in the room. I fell down to my knees. My only option was to crawl to the stairs.

"Larissa." Yelling, I waited down there like a damn invalid for her to come help my ass. Listening, I waited a few more minutes. *Shit.* The shower was running. The queen of forty-five-minute showers would not be coming to help my ass anytime soon. My eyes were rolling in my head every time I tried to look in any given direction, and, I mean, I'd had vertigo before, but never to this extreme. I pulled myself up the stairs one at a time, surprised I made it all the way to the bedroom without puking before I collapsed in the middle of the bed. The last thing I remembered was jasmine soap and body oil while Larissa stood over me, naked and wet, looking down at me, drying her hair with a towel. And then there was nothing.

CHAPTER 9

DON'T BE EYEBALLIN' ME, MISTER

Hopefully this date would be more exciting than the last one. It was late, midnight when the car came to get me, and my ass was tired but ready to make this money. Lania said this dude was into some kinda kinky bondage-type shit so I put on an all-black cat suit. She was like he usually just be on some step on his balls or paddle his ass type of craziness that I ain't know people really paid for, but as long as I ain't have to fuck him, it was whatever.

The car let me out in front of nice hotel no more than twenty minutes from the house. This was a little too close to home for my taste, but Nino, this big-ass Italian muscle gorilla—looking muthafucka, one of Lania's bodyguards, would be outside if I needed him and would be followin' me back home, so fuck it, I was all in. Nino escorted me through the lobby up to room 376. He stood a few feet down the hall away from the door so he wouldn't scare the client. Knockin' on the door, I took a couple breaths 'cause I noticed my hand was shakin'. The door swung open and a tall shirtless white guy was standin' there. He was tan as fuck. I mean so tan he looked brown and all the hair on his chest and on his head looked white.

"How you doin', beautiful?" He had a friendly smile that made me feel comfortable, so I smiled back and walked in. He offered me a drink but I turned it down as I was instructed.

"What would you like to do, um . . ." Embarrassed, I realized I couldn't remember his damn name.

"Call me Leslie."

I stared at him, 'cause I wasn't sure if that was part of his fetish, but I was damn sure Leslie was a woman's name.

"It's a unisex name, darlin'."

Damn can this muthafucka read minds, too? I besta stop thinkin'.

"Well okay then, Leslie, you can call me Trista." I made it up and cringed. I coulda come up with somethin' better than that, but oh well.

"Okay, Trista. That's fine an' dandy but I'ma call you Chocolate Thai. Now, c'mere. Take your clothes off."

Did this bitch . . . I wasn't sure if I was supposed to be offended or if that was a racial thing, and, *naked? I could have sworn Lania said he don't do sex.*

"C'mon now, Chocolate Thai. I ain't got all night."

"But, Leslie, I'm sure they told you I don't have sex, right?" I was still close enough to the door that I could run my ass up outta there if I needed to.

"I'm sure they told you I like *other* things. Now. Naked. Here. Please."

He stripped down to his ugly-ass tighty whities and lay across the bed and, fuck, if I ain't feel stuck between a damn couple thousand and a hard Leslie. I took my shit off, gritting my teeth the whole time all the way down to my damn draws. If this fool tried to slide anything up in anywhere, I swear I was screamin' for Nino so damn fast.

"Now, come over here, beautiful, and lemme see what Chocolate Thai taste like." Ladies and gentlemen, when this fool said he wanted to see what it taste like,

I kid you not . . . Climbin' up on the bed, I'm preppin' myself to ask his ass if he got a dental dam or some shit, 'cause he wasn't 'bout to be puttin' his mouth all over my pussy unprotected. Before I could get the words out he scooped my ass up—y'all know I'm small—and had me squattin' over his face so he could rub his eyes, *yes, his eyes,* all up in my stuff. I could feel him blinkin' and shit. His eyelashes were tickling the fuck outta me an' I was tryin' not to laugh while I just *squatted* there. His free hand was in his draws strokin' away and I was just perched up there lookin' around like *what the fuck kinda freak nasty shit is this?*

Easiest $8,000 I've ever made in my entire life.

CHAPTER 10

GIVING ME HEAD ... ACHES

Wakin' up was hell. It felt like my arms and legs were disconnected from my head and my torso. I was all kinds of groggy and couldn't remember why. Larissa and I hadn't spoken more than a few words to each other since Saturday night and not only was she being an asshole, but she was doing it in the most frustrating ways possible. Aside from her time with the kids she spent almost every day walking around the damn house butt-ass naked. I swear the woman was intentionally boycotting her damn clothing. There were times when I'd have to literally tell myself to close my mouth and stop staring. I was so sexually frustrated, I knew for a fact if you put me on a treadmill hooked up to a generator I could provide enough power to run half of Miami for at least a week. I was also having to either cook or order something because most of the time, aside from some tea or a sandwich, she was refusing to cook or lift a finger and I was starting to get beyond fed up with her bullshit.

Every day I'd been home from work on time and today would be the first day that I'd be late. I'd met with Jim Bartell from Strong Arm Security. Until Rah or whoever decided to show their face it just seemed like the logical thing to do. Jim was a much older white man with a leathery tan face, head full of white hair, and the clearest blue eyes I'd ever seen. He made it a point to come meet me at my office in case I was being followed. He didn't want to raise any suspicion or draw the attention of whoever was harassing us. My meeting with him was a blur of paperwork and certifications, where I pretty much put the protection of my life and those of the Ris and the kids at the mercy of his security team. It cost an arm and a leg but knowing that I'd have someone at the house around the clock in addition to someone trailing me wherever I went was a definite relief.

I'd purposefully been ignoring texts and phone calls from both Keyshawn *and* Lania. Their persistence was damn amazing. If the roles were reversed I'd have given up on myself by Tuesday. I was leaving the office as usual when my phone went off. It was a text from Keyshawn:

It's Thursday, haven't heard from you. Dinner party @ Curtis' place Friday 9. Hope you're a woman of your word. Would be honored if you'd make an appearance. Bring wifey if you're feelin' scary.

Damn. The nigga knew how to get my attention. I drove the rest of the way home silently debating whether I should stay or go, take Ris or leave her. There were just so many variables to consider. Was Lania going to be there? Was his entourage of random hoes going to be there? If I asked Key about any of them would it come across as strange? Would Lania act funny toward me since I'd pretty much shut her down and been brushing her off ever since?

My phone vibrated again but it was Jim calling from the security company. I'd been waiting to hear back from him since setting everything up on Monday.

"Answer call." I rarely used the in-car mobile audio feature but figured I'd might as well since I had it. "This is Michelle."

"Michelle, this is Jim. How are ya?"

I smiled when I heard his heavy Southern accent; he sounded like a straight-up farm-raised country boy. "I'm doing well thank you."

"Good. I've been looking into yer situation. The bad news is Rasheed is no longer in custody in Virginia."

My vision momentarily blacked out. If I weren't sitting in traffic I might have crashed, or run off the highway at the sound of those words.

"Rasheed isn't what? You mean transferred? Right? Jim?" I couldn't even form a complete coherent sentence.

"Well now, Michelle, I mean escaped."

The depth of meaning behind those words alone threatened to swallow me alive.

"Apparently three weeks ago a female CO helped him escape. She's been missing in action ever since. Suspected to either be out on the run with him or paid 'nuff to disappear. Put him in a K-9 trainin' unit cage—pretended he was a sick dog, needed to see a vet. Guards on duty were useless pricks, didn't even bother checkin' the crate as required. She drove him out in the mornin'—they ain' know 'til they did the night count." My mind was reeling. God I felt like I was gonna be sick. I fought the urge to vomit and waited for Jim to continue. My worst nightmare was coming true.

"Now don't panic. I want you to go 'bout yer business an' keep livin' as you normally would. Possum only play possum 'til you walk away. So we don't want him to know we watchin' you or the li'l ones."

Did this muthafucka just say, "don't panic"? I almost hysterically laughed out loud. He obviously didn't know how calculating Rah was when it came to getting his revenge.

"Rasheed is a very dangerous man, Jim. As I told you before he's just tormentin' me right now. His revenge is never a pretty or fair thing."

"I read his file, seen his face, I know what he's done. My boys know exactly who they're lookin' fer an' what kinda man they're dealin' with. We've protected folk from much more dangerous people than yer ordinary street thug, ma'am. All I'ma do is double up on yer security an' there's no extra charge fer that. There's already a wanted bulletin out fer him across all states from Virginia all the way down here. The reward to turn 'im in is bigger than the payout fer helpin' his ass, I can assure you that much."

All the blood had drained from my hands, my grip was so tight on the steering wheel. I removed them and tried flexing my fingers. I took a few deep breaths and tried focusing on the traffic as it began to move ahead.

"Jim? I need somewhere to take my children. He isn't going to want to hurt the kids. It's jus' me an' my wife he's really after. Do you have anywhere, like a safe house?" My voice was shaky from fear and from the tears I was fighting back. I refused to cry. I got myself into this shit, and I'd fight my way the fuck out of it.

"Well yes, ma'am. I've got a few places—quieter than gerbil piss on cotton if ya know what I mean. They're well off the grid, very limited access. Gonna take a li'l time tho'—gotta get y'all all clear. In the meantime please try ta relax. You hired some of *the* best men in the business, I swear on my own life. Summa my boys are retired Seals, Secret Service, and CIA. We ain't lost a client yet and I don't plan on losin' one anytime soon, baby doll."

I tried to find the reassurance that Jim was offering. He sounded like an overprotective older grandfather, talking to me like I'd just skinned my knee. But this was no skinned knee and I wasn't his granddaughter; to him I was just another dollar. Shit, another couple thousand dollars a day, but you get my damn point.

"All right, Jim, I'm not gonna panic. I'm gonna do my best to trust you on this." I was saying it more to convince myself than to convince him.

"That's good, sweetheart. Now if you have any events, attend 'em as usual. We want to draw this summa bitch out. You sittin' up in the house ain' gonna do it."

"Really! You want me to do what?" What he was suggesting went against every molecular instinct in my body. The last thing I wanted to do was leave the safety of my home, not after knowing for a fact Rah was out and most likely out for blood.

"Sweetheart, I been doin' this pro'ly since you were in pigtails. When's all the stuff been happenin' that you told me 'bout—when you were goin' or comin', right?"

I sighed and it felt like the longest, most drawn-out damn sigh I'd ever sighed in my entire life. He did have a point. Everything happened when I wasn't in the house. If this was what they needed in order to draw him out and haul his ass back to prison, all I could do was shake my head.

"All right, Jim. My wife and I have a dinner party to attend tomorrow evening with Keyshawn the basketball player. Unless she decides not to go, then it'll just be me by myself." By this point fear literally had me shaking from head to toe; it was like I'd just jumped out of a tub of ice water. I turned on the seat warmer, hoping it would help me regain some of my composure.

"No problem, ma'am. I believe one my boys said they'd seen him stop by the house one day. But the other miss talked with him so there seemed to be no problem. Just call me with yer itinerary before you leave. Jus' lemme know where yer headed, an' what time, an' the information fer the sitter who'll be keepin' the kids while yer gone. We'll handle the rest."

"Okay, thank you." I disconnected the call and pulled over to the side of the highway, on to the shoulder for vehicle breakdowns. All of this had to be a bad dream. At any minute Ris would kiss me and wake me up and everything would be back to normal. I was momentarily stunned. *And Keyshawn was at the house? He talked to Ris? Why?* The only thing that came to mind was that he was looking for me, since I hadn't been answering any of his messages. I just hoped he'd made something up good enough to convince Ris of why he'd stop by unannounced.

My mind was overloaded. I couldn't fight my tears anymore. Technically this was a breakdown, just not a mechanical one. I was freezing in the middle of summer, scared, and I had no idea if I could go through with this shit. I jumped as something hit the driver-side window hard and loud. It was a younger white guy with dusky blond hair, wearing dark sunglasses. I was afraid to roll down my window and only cracked it slightly.

"Yes?" I barely croaked out the word and tried to find something to wipe my nose with.

"Ma'am, Strong Arm Security. I'm Keith."

I breathed a sigh of relief. Keith pointed at the hood of my car. To anyone watching it would appear as if he were just a Good Samaritan asking if I was having car trouble.

"You need not be stoppin' on the highway like this. Are you okay?"

I sniffled loudly and shook my head yes.

"All right, I'm gonna radio in for a switch in case my vehicle's been compromised. But I'm right here until my relief arrives."

"I'm sorry, okay. Thank you." I pulled myself together and put the car into drive, feeling slightly secure with my paid guardian angel trailing me.

The rest of the drive home I was on auto pilot as I silently debated exactly what Ris needed to know. It wouldn't be fair to hide something like this from her but I had two things to consider. Ris already thought I was doing wrong by her and this would further fuel her bullshit misconceptions. Her track record for dealing with Rasheed stress has always been to use and I definitely didn't want to start her on that path again. It would make the most sense for her to go with me to the party, if I could convince her. With us both out of the house I would at least know my babies were okay. After what happened with Derrick, and Rasheed's oldest son, I could almost bet every dollar to my name that he wouldn't dare touch the kids.

Ris and I were the targets. If we kept ourselves busy and away from the kids then hopefully Rah would surface and everything would play itself out. By the time I pulled into my driveway my mind was completely made up. My hands were shaking so bad I could barely type Key's name into my directory to pull up his information.

Send me Curtis' address. Rsvp +1 thanks Chelle.

I sat there with the car still running, trying to pull myself together while I waited for his reply.

Gotcha Lady. 1610 Medallion Arch Miami see you there ;)

I knew the area very well; some of the wealthiest people in Florida had properties in that area. I called to see if Darla was available and called Jim back with all of the information he'd requested before going into the house. I didn't want Ris listening in on anything that would alarm her.

"So we gotta have private convos in the car now?"

Where the fuck did she come from? I wasn't even a good two steps in the door before Ris was in front of me, splendidly naked and pissed the fuck off, eyes glaring up at me—hands on her hips.

"Damn, so we spy out of windows now? We don't speak for an entire week, and these are the first words we say to someone who gets us an exclusive invite to a party with the owner of Keyshawn's team?" I glared down at her, my own anger fueled by my stress.

"Fuck a party. Who da hell were you out there talkin' to dat you couldn't talk in da damn house?"

Wow, she was fuming. That's the best word for anger that I could think of to accurately describe a Ris who wouldn't get excited over a party. As if on cue, the kids came bursting downstairs as they always did. They were oblivious to Ris's lack of clothing, letting me know she'd most likely been like that all damn day. I knelt down and kissed both my babies on the tops of their heads, wondering why they were still in their PJs. She at least could have washed them up and put clothes on they asses.

"Hey my loves, Mommy and I need to talk, go play upstairs. Are you guys hungry?" They both yelled yes in unison, and I rolled my eyes. She apparently hadn't bothered fixing them anything to eat either.

"Okay, go upstairs and I'll call you when it's ready." I waited until they were both out of sight. I stared down at her and tried to be as understanding as I could, but my patience was wearing thin. "Larissa, are you on something?"

"The fuck kinda . . . No. Um, Michelle, are you on somebody dick when you ain't up in dis house?"

I had to count to ten twice before I could speak. "No, Ris. I didn't wanna scare the kids. I hired a security company to watch all of us. There's a unit that follows me and there's another one that will stay wherever you and the kids are. That's who I was on the phone with. I also called and got Darla for tomorrow because I assumed you'd wanna go with me to Curtis's party."

Her face softened up just slightly even though I could still see the doubt in her eyes. I walked into the living room and sat on the couch, pulling the security contract out of my briefcase. I held it out in one hand and just let it hang there. She was no more than a few steps behind me and it wasn't long before she took it from my extended hand and started reading it over. I knew her entirely too well.

"Damn, bae, this shit is expensive."

Inwardly I rolled my eyes, thinking, *no shit.* "Our lives are worth way more than that, Ris."

She dropped down onto the couch beside me and didn't say a word. Not a "thank you," "I'm sorry," nothing.

"Do we really need someone watchin' us all like this? I think you're overreacting. Why didn't you discuss this with me first? I feel like a prisoner bein' followed an' spied on without my permission."

"Ris, you're lookin' at it for the wrong reasons. It's not personal. It's for protection." I couldn't believe she was actually taking offense to having someone watch out for her. I swore when it came to this woman I could never do anything right no matter how hard I tried.

"So when you say they signed confidentiality agreements, that means that they keep our shit private? They just protect us and go about they business."

"That's exactly what it means. And what's up with this sudden aversion you've taken to wearin' your damn clothes?"

"Huh? Oh, um nothin' I jus' ain' feel like puttin' any on one day or the next. So I didn't. So what time is this party we s'posed to be hittin' up?"

Relief swept over me like a cool breeze hitting the desert sand. I leaned forward and kissed Ris's shoulder, expecting her to pull away, but she didn't. I rested my lips there and closed my eyes, inhaling her warm jasmine-vanilla scent that was so familiar to me. I couldn't help myself; it had been too long and I'd been teased and toyed with too many times over the last couple of days. Something needed to take my mind off of all the drama and craziness. Ris was so petite and easy to maneuver, it was nothing for me to grab her and pull her in closer to me. For her to be walking around completely naked she was still amazingly warm and her body heat ignited me—soothing me at the same time.

You know something? Every woman has a tell. The shit works just like poker. No matter how pissed off she was or how indifferent she tried to act—her tell would give her away every single time. I licked my lips and lightly floated a warm, wet kiss from the base of her neck down all the way down to the small of her back, and instinctively she arched. That was Ris's tell. I smiled a devilish smile. I had her.

"Chelle, let's go upstairs." That small action had her voice in an almost breathless whisper. She ain't have to tell me twice. I kicked off my heels and was off the couch before she could even stand up. We tiptoed past the kids' room; they were playing and wouldn't remember they were hungry for at least another hour or so. When we made it to our bedroom, Ris surprised me by pushing me up against the bedroom door and standing on her toes to kiss me. I closed my eyes, enjoying the fullness of her lips and the giving in her kiss. Ris always kissed as if she were kissing with her very soul. Her naked body pressed tightly against me, she could take my take my breath away just with the earnest genuine love and passion in her kisses. My hands began to frantically remove my clothing, desperate to feel the fire of her skin pressed against mine.

"Bae, I've missed you *so much*. I'm so sorry." Her lips broke from mine and she whispered in between kissing each little area of skin I uncovered, and I couldn't get my blazer, blouse, or my skirt off fast enough. We fell onto the bed in a tangle with Ris landing on top of me. I closed my eyes as the heat of her mouth circled and teased one nipple. Her mouth left my skin just long enough to circle and give the same attention to its twin. I was trying my damnedest not to think about cherries or rosé. I reached down with both hands and roughly cupped her ass, making her moan in response, and I silently cursed. It wasn't the same as that hoarse, deep, sultry sound Lania made. Ris ventured farther down my body, her tongue burning a path that just couldn't seem to melt my icy exterior. I needed to stop her before she found disappointment in the fact that she was putting in all this work and I wasn't wet yet.

I started to reach down and stop her but I was surprised when she stopped on her own.

"Remember when I said I had a trick for you?"

I was half excited and half scared to answer her. She didn't need an answer. I stared at the bounce in her ass as she hopped up and disappeared into her closet. She quickly came back with a black bag and a blindfold. Cautiously I started to sit up.

"I know you better not have a damn snake or no crazy shit." I was dead-ass serious. Ris was unpredictable sometimes and I'd be damned if she thought we were gonna play animal kingdom up in here. She giggled and kissed me, kneeling over me blindfold in hand.

"No, baby, it's nothing like dat. I ain't even gonna tie you up or nothin', so you can stop me at any time. Okay?"

I reluctantly nodded, and let her engulf me in darkness as she placed the blindfold over my eyes and climbed off of me.

"Turn on your stomach, bae."

I did as instructed. Without being able to see, my senses were heightened beyond reason. The heat from Ris's body seemed to magnify as she lay fully on my back and gently nibbled at my tell—my neck. I couldn't help it. Any and all thoughts of Lania suddenly vanished as the scent of jasmine and Ris's body heat took over my senses.

She gently sucked at one side of my neck, letting me enjoy the feel of the heat from her mouth before she slid her lips across the nape of my neck to do the same to the other. She made it a point to only lightly graze me with her teeth. Teasing me. Her hands were liquid heat as they slid underneath me to tug and tease at my nipples, twirling them between her warm fingers. I tilted my head to give her lips better access and damn near screamed when suddenly her teeth sank deep into the sensitive spot between my shoulder and collarbone.

I was lost. I could feel myself starting to throb for attention. Her hands were everywhere as she trailed kisses down my sides and my back. She softly nibbled and kissed my ass and my thighs, making me squirm impatiently. We'd never played this game before so I honestly had no idea what to expect. She left me for a second and I could hear the bag rustling as I waited. Unexpected shivers ran all the up my spine that vibrated behind my eyelids when suddenly her nose parted my ass and her tongue drove deep into my pussy from behind, causing me to nearly arch off the bed.

Larissa had *never* done that before. I buried my face into the comforter and prayed it muffled my moans. The heat from her tongue was driving me crazy. She made lazy circles back and forth up and around my clit, teasing and prodding. Ris moaned, and I melted, soaking the comforter and all the bedding underneath. She was lapping up every drop and thoroughly enjoying it. I was so damn close my legs were starting to shake.

"Mmm somebody been eatin' they pineapples. You ready, bae?"

Damn right, I thought, because my ass couldn't talk. She was mumbling with her mouth full, but I still understood her. I was so far gone I couldn't even answer. But oh yes, I was definitely ready. I wiggled my ass farther back onto her nose and tongue as my reply. I could feel the first throb, the first convulsion. I hadn't cum in so long I'd stopped keeping track. Sparks and flashes were starting to appear behind the blindfold due to me squeezing my eyes closed so tight. The comforter was now gripped between my teeth and I was on a downward spiral straight into—*shock!* My eyes widened behind the blindfold. I gasped as every good feeling suddenly fled from me as quickly as it had approached. *No this heffa did not just jam her muthafuckin finger in my damn ass.*

"What the fuck?" I bucked forward. Pain, anger, and just a tinge of feel good still coursed through my system. Her finger was still jammed firmly in place like that little Dutch girl you see in all those pictures plugging the leak in the dam.

"Bae, come back. I said I had a trick for you, damn. It's s'posed to make you cum harder." She sounded aggravated.

I stared back at her, wide-eyed and in complete shock while I tried to relax around the sudden unexpected intrusion in my damn asshole.

"Damn, Larissa, you could've prepped it first. Licked your finger, lubed it up with some K-Y, I don't know." I mentally analyzed my asshole for a second. Surprisingly, it wasn't as bad as I thought it'd be, it was actually kind of tingly. A little numbness seemed to be spreading around, but it sure wasn't super fantastic either.

"I did. What do you think was in the bag? Now come back."

I tried to relax but there was just something "dirty" feeling about anus play and I couldn't help it. I kept clenching my ass cheeks and making the stank face at her. Ris had officially with a single finger killed the moment, and all the blood rushing from my head back up to my head was starting to make me feel lightheaded.

"Ris, you done killed it. I'm good—I can't."

"Mommmmmy." The sound of our voices obviously reminded the kids of the fact that they hadn't been fed and they both chimed in, screaming from outside the bedroom door. Ris actually surprised me for once.

"I'll go, and I'll bring you somethin' for your head." She gently slid her index finger out of my ass and I cringed. *Damn, she could've at least started with a pinky. Where they do that at?*

"Ris," I called after her when she was halfway out the door. "Please wash that thing before you feed my babies."

She wiggled it at me and I leaned back in horror, frustration at yet again *almost* getting off completely pissing me off. Yeah, I definitely felt a headache coming on.

CHAPTER 11

WORKIN' WOMAN

"Taya, sit yo' li'l yella ass down befo' I sit you down."

She stared at me, her eyes all round and shit like she ain't know what I was saying. I gave her a 3.2-second window to drop back down into her little pink plastic chair; otherwise, I was gonna light her ass up. Dropping peanut butter and jelly sandwiches onto the table in front of the kids, I pulled out my cell.

"Don't neitha of y'all move 'til I come back. Mommy is upstairs sleeping. I don't wanna hear a damn peep. Okay?"

They both nodded at me slowly.

"Now eat." I walked out into the garage, sweat beading up on my forehead instantly. *Shit, Michelle so good for heating up floors and wasting money on security and shit, why we can't put air conditioning in the damn garage?* That seemed to be where I was spending so much of my spare time any damn way.

"Ahhh, hey, you. I just got feedback, a complaint from Darnell, who was not very pleased. You do know that, right?" Lania was talking small shit right now.

I already had Darnell's money so I couldn't care less what he was or wasn't happy 'bout.

"Shit, you didn't tell me I needed to take a case of Tic Tacs with me. I might've made a necklace out of mints or offered that nigga some Binaca first."

"Well, Mr. Leslie loved you and Darnell is always hard to please. Plus, I had to know how you would handle not-so-pleasant or beautiful situations. Darnell was like an initiation, you did well, though."

Well damn, let me find out this heffa got herself a mini sorority and shit. I shuddered, a chill of disgust running through my body at just the thought of Darnell's breath on the side of my face.

"Well I'm callin' you 'cause I got a bigger problem. Michelle ass done went out and hired a security company to fuckin' follow us around and shit. Not regular security. These niggas in unmarked cars doin' hidden surveillance-type shit."

The line was quiet for a minute. I could tell I had Lania stumped with that one. Hell, my ass was stumped too.

"Hmm, security company you say? We will have to think on this little hiccup. I'm sure there are ways around her hired dogs. Enough bullshit, are you guys coming to the party?"

"She mentioned a dinner party or somethin' but I don't know. We got a lot goin' on right now."

"Oh trust me we have the best parties, best coke, best everything. If she's worried about security Curtis has his own. No one's going to come up in there with any shit. I might also have something for you, if you feel like making some *extra money*."

Her emphasis on the words "extra money" let me know plain and simple this wouldn't be a regular meet-and-greet type situation.

"I know how you are about men, this one would definitely be different."

The thought of making another five or eight grand had my heart going triple time. That would put me at damn near $20,000 in less than a week. At this rate

I'd be making so much money I wouldn't even need to worry about Michelle taking care of me, or leaving me anymore. I couldn't resist it. "All right, I'm in. What do you need me to do?"

"I'll fill you in when you get to the party, and then we'll have to find a way to get you away from your wifey. I promise we will have so much fun—even your uptight Michelle will be drunk dancing by the time we're all done."

I almost laughed in Lania's damn ear trying to picture that shit happening. *Never in a million years, no—no way—no how.*

"Lania, you obviously don't know my wife."

CHAPTER 12

DOUBLE TAKE

Darla showed up right on time as expected and I led her upstairs to the playroom where the kids were quietly watching a movie. Ris was still in the bathroom, getting dressed. I smoothed an imaginary wrinkle out of the burgundy and gold comforter on our bed and sat down. I'd decided to keep my attire simple, wearing a black high-waist Cavalli pencil skirt and my favorite silver Yves Saint Laurent blouse that flared at my collarbone. It was sexy, yet classy; with the right pair of glasses I could definitely pull off the naughty librarian image.

I was too antsy and stressed out to worry about fussing over my hair. Instead, I opted to just let it hang loose, falling past my shoulders with the ends bumped under so it curled slightly. I might have looked like a perfectly composed, well put together woman on the outside but, on the inside, I was a complete and absolute mess.

Nothing was adding up. I was so careful when we left Virginia. I'd gone through so much trouble getting us away from there as quickly as possible and as discretely as possible. How on earth had Rah managed to find us? The question rolled over in my head repeatedly along with the image of his face the last time I'd seen him. Years hadn't erased that memory: the day he realized that the misery he'd suffer for the rest of his life was all because of us, because of me. There was so much hate and anger.

My stomach had rumbled very loudly, interrupting my thoughts. I hadn't had much of an appetite since talking to Jim, and Lord knows I couldn't eat anything. My nerves were so bad I constantly felt nauseous. A few strong drinks were exactly what I needed, but just enough to calm my nerves so I could talk business with Curtis if the opportunity presented itself.

"I'm all ready." Ris walked in looking like she was going to either a rap video or porn shoot audition. She was wearing her bright pink "come fuck me" stilettos, the ones we only used for playing dress-up. They were paired with a matching skirt and matching see-through fishnet top with a black and pink zebra-striped bra underneath.

"Um, you know this is a dinner party and not a Nicki Minaj lookalike contest right?" I was agitated and didn't bother hiding it.

"Oh whateva. If you wanna roll up in there lookin' like somebody's damn principal dat's on you. I seen how Key an' his people do on TV, my ass gon' fit right the fuck in. Watch."

And watch was exactly what I'd decided to do. The gated mansion community was nothing like the ones Ris had ever been exposed to. We'd been to mansion parties in Virginia, but trying to compare a million dollar house to a multi-million dollar estate is about the same as trying to compare Section 8 housing to Executive Condos. They ain't even in the same playing field.

When the limo dropped us off in front of the main entrance my own eyes widened; this man's house was the size of a small strip mall. There had to be at least five levels to it on the inside. A butler greeted us, carrying a tray of champagne, and we each took glasses. It was nine o'clock on the dot and I imagined we must have been the first to arrive, seeing as how there were no other cars in front, unless he had a damn parking garage somewhere that I just hadn't seen. It was highly fucking possible.

We were led inside through the main foyer by another suited-up butler. It reminded me of the Roman Colosseum in Italy where the gladiators fought. Huge pillars lined both sides and Ris and I both stopped and looked up in awe. The ceiling was hundreds of feet up, but instead of the typical chandelier the ceiling was a constellation of glittering stars and planets, and every so often a shooting star would fly from one end of the ceiling across to the other.

"The guests are all in the evening ballroom. Follow me please."

I was so busy staring at the place, I'd completely forgotten about the butler.

Ris giggled and downed her glass of champagne. "Follow Alfred."

I rolled my eyes at her immature comment. We walked past statues of Hercules, Apollo, and other Greek gods. Curtis seemed to have a serious thing for power figures. We were led down several long hallways before finally stopping in front of an elevator.

"You are going to the fourth floor, enjoy."

We stepped inside and Ris and I both looked at each other, eyes as wide as saucers. "This nigga got a muthafuckin' elevator *in his house,*" we said in unison, giggling on the way up. I immediately felt transported into another world. The doors opened up and before us was what I'm just going to call "Club Curtis." This fool had a disco ball and everything. The entire fourth floor was Curtis's own private club, DJ booth and all. The area was darkened with multicolored strobe lights flashing overhead. I squinted and looked through the crowd of people blocking the elevator entrance, trying to find Keyshawn's ass. Ris nudged me in my ribs when a top-less waitress walked by with a tray of syringe-shaped shooters and multicolored Jell-O shots.

"I told yo' ass I'd fit the fuck in, Ms. Know-it-fuckin'-all."

I just ignored her.

"Hey hey hey, *mi* gorgeous, momma's glad you both could make it." Lania swirled out of thin air, pulling me into a hug that lasted a little too long for my taste, which ended with her air-kissing me on either side of my face. She was obviously already a few shots or champagne glasses ahead of us. She then turned and pulled Ris into the same embrace.

"I just love, love, love you in these color. Perfect pink like pussy is, yes?"

"Well fuck yes," Ris chimed back, obviously happy someone else agreed with the outfit that my ass so openly disapproved of.

Oh well isn't this just wonderful. Here I was look-ing like the Nutty Professor's assistant and every-one—including Lania, in her see-through, barely there, all-white body suit—was in straight-up hoochie wear. Keyshawn approached us, his smile already preparing me for the damn jokes.

"Hmm, now did I say come to a party or come defend me in court?"

I glared and he laughed, making me blush. We hugged and I couldn't help but notice he was wearing Vera Wang for Men cologne, and damn it if that shit didn't smell good. I bit my bottom lip. He escorted us over to the bar and I tried to get the attention of the topless bartender.

"I know this heffa sees me standing here." I blamed my damn outfit.

Key walked up behind me and ordered us all shots of Patrón Platinum and mojitos as chasers from a man who looked like one of the statues I'd seen in the hallway who was also tending the bar.

"Curtis. You remember Michelle and Larissa right?"

I turned and extended my hand but was instead pulled into a tight bear hug that damn near took my breath away.

"Sure as hell do. Beautiful women I never forget."

We exchanged minor small talk over our drinks.

"What the fuck is this?" Key's comment was directed toward the elevator as Curtis walked over to meet the new arrivals. They exchanged hugs before walking back over to our little gathering.

"I'd like to introduce you all to Angelo Testa. This is Michelle and her wife."

It was the same man from the club earlier with his entourage of women. I'd seen them disperse to different parts of the room as Curtis brought him over to meet us. He was a beautiful, younger-looking Italian man to say the least, with piercing grey eyes that looked like they could see straight through you. I reached out to shake his hand and he grabbed mine, turning it over in his and softly kissing the inside of my wrist instead.

"Absolutely beautiful. Such a shame."

"Why, because I'm married or because I like women?" I stared back at him, waiting for his answer. His gaze was making me nervous as he stared up at me. I thought it was the intensity in those grey eyes of his that made me uneasy. He opened his mouth as if he were about to answer me and was distracted as Keyshawn slammed his glass down. The glass shattered as it hit the bar and Keyshawn walked toward the elevator with disgust written all over his face.

Angelo turned to Lania, who'd come up to give him a hug.

"You should tell your people ova' there to be more respectful, need I remind him of his place on the totem pole?"

"Please don't mind Keyshawn, he's been drinking. The champagne you sent over at LIV was wonderful, by the way."

I listened to Lania and Angelo, but I was still looking in the direction Keyshawn had gone. I couldn't help but feel like there was something more to Key's behavior than just the liquor.

"Is he going to be playing at his best or should I be concerned? I have a great deal of assets in play right now—I don't want his dick getting in the way of his focus." Angelo motioned for one of his girls to come over while waiting for Lania to answer his question.

Lania looked anxiously in the direction that Keyshawn had just walked in and gave me a nervous, apologetic smile that I tried to return. *I guess basketball is that serious of a business in these parts.*

"He'll play, Angelo, don't you worry about him. I'll handle it, I always do. You have my word." There was sadness in Lania's voice and I couldn't help but wonder what the hell was going on with these three.

By the end of the night my ass was done. The room was completely spinning and all I could do was sit my ass down and watch everyone else. Drinking on an empty stomach was such a fucking bad idea. The crowd had started thinning out and I could only see a few people scattered here and there throughout the huge area. Ris was laughing and dancing with Lania and Chanel. I dizzily scanned the room for Keyshawn, but he was nowhere to be found. I only closed my eyes for what felt like a split second. When I opened them, Lania was lying in the floor, covered in what appeared to be blood. My head throbbed as I tried to get up. Curtis and several others were hovering over here. Ris, to no surprise, had vanished.

"Curtis. What . . . what happened?" Fear sobered me up quick as fuck. *Did Ris do this shit?* I was scared to even speak the words out of my mouth. She had a jealous streak, mean, and a crazy streak. Ignite all three and hell would certainly break loose. I kneeled beside Lania looking for a puncture wound, squinting at her face for signs of a fight, but saw none.

"Don't stand y'all asses there. Somebody get a towel. Did anybody call nine-one-one?" I was frantic. At least if she survived it wouldn't be considered manslaughter. There were too many witnesses to keep this one under wraps. Frustrated, I look around. Nobody was moving fast enough to make me happy and I hopped up, sending the room reeling around me.

"Nah. Think she just fainted. That ain't blood; she was drinkin' her umpteenth Bloody Mary. My guess is she done did too much of that shit and not enough water. Got a doc on the way. He said don't move her." It was Curtis who answered and he was so calm, like this kind of shit happened all the time. I looked around again and still saw no sign of Ris.

"Did too much of what shit, Curtis?"

"Oh hell pills, coke, new shit, who knows."

Immediately I started worrying. If Lania had access to anything, Ris did too. The last time I'd seen her they were together. Clumsily I made my way to the elevator and pushed three, two, and one. When it stopped on the third floor I got off in a dimly lit hallway. The first door I came to was a large sauna. Head spinning, I heard faint laughter coming from the other end of the hallway. It sounded like Keyshawn, but I wasn't sure. *If Ris is off somewhere fuckin' this muthafucka, I swear on my life and everything I own and have ever had I will kill them both without a second thought, right on the muthafuckin' spot.*

As I neared the door toward the end of the hall I could now clearly hear Ris and Keyshawn. I instantly saw, for the first time in my life, what I've heard people call "white rage." I tested the doorknob and my heart damn near beat out of my chest when I found that it was unlocked. Twisting the knob ever so slowly, I tried to open it without making a sound. My blood ran cold at the sound of Ris's voice.

"Oh my God, Key, I didn't know I was missin' all this!" Breathless and excited, her voice was a high-pitched squeal of delight. That was a Ris I hadn't heard in forever and it hurt that I wasn't the reason for her excitement.

"Yeah, baby! I know, I know. It take a *real nigga* to show you how this shit get done!" Keyshawn's conceited ass was just as out of breath.

That was it; I saw pure blood red. Bursting through the door like a bull blindly charging a matador I ran into the room. Tears were already starting to run down my face from the pain, and anger, but mostly from Ris's disloyalty. I cursed myself for not having a fucking pistol or a knife or anything with me. In my rage I decided to just beat their asses to death with my bare hands if I had to. I saw Keyshawn first and blindly lunged toward him.

"What the fuck, Key? This is how you do huh? You come at me an' talk all that shit an'. . ." I launched, my body set on full-all-out attack mode.

I was on him before the fact that he was fully clothed and standing in front of the TV beside Ris, who was also fully clothed, registered. All of that filtered through long after I'd already embarrassed myself.

"Michelle? You on something, ma? You good?" He'd grabbed both of my wrists, restraining me like I was nothing but a rag doll, looking me in my eyes as if he were trying to see if my pupils were dilated.

"I'm fuckin' fine. Let me go, damn."

Ris was beside him, staring at me wide-eyed. I couldn't help standing there feeling like a complete fucking idiot.

"Baby, we was just playin' this dance game on Curtis's Xbox. You were asleep upstairs an' I didn't wanna wake you up. Curtis said it was okay to jus' leave you be 'til e'rebody left."

Deflated, I dragged myself over to the humongous bed off to the side, suddenly feeling like I'd just poured all of my energy out in that fit of idiocy. I sat on the edge, my head down and my shoulders slumped in embarrassment.

"I'm jus' kin'a wasted, a li'l maybe. I think." Damn, and I was slurring. I could hear them laughing as I fell back exhausted from not sleeping, not eating, worrying about way too much, and taking way too many shots.

It must have been close to 3:00 A.M. when I was awakened from my liquor/exhaustion-induced coma to the feeling of warm lips running laps around my nipples. I tried to open my eyes but the room spun like crazy so I closed them and let myself relax. Fresh Jasmine caressed my senses and immediately I knew it was Ris. I moaned when she did that thing I love so much: lightly grazing the sensitive skin around my breast with her teeth. I was still too damn drunk to do much more than just lie there.

The combination of liquor and grogginess were working to her advantage. She was talking to me but I couldn't make out the words. I tried to focus. Cool air hit my skin and I realized I was completely naked. The bedroom was dim and I couldn't tell if it was from candlelight or light dimmers. Ris hovered over me, all of her clothing gone, leaving her completely naked, completely beautiful. Her eyes reflected the lighting as she looked down at me. They also reflected something else. I wasn't quite sure what it was, but it was sexy. She leaned down and kissed me softly before whispering in my ear.

"Baby, I told them they could watch us."

I didn't know what "them" she was talking about. I gazed around as best as I could without making the room move again. I wasn't able to focus. Ris climbed up, straddling me; she was already hot, soaking wet. I could feel the heat and her moisture pressing against my stomach. Suddenly the thought of someone somewhere watching was the last thing on my mind. I blinked, trying to regain my bearings, hoping it would stop the spinning in my head.

In one fluid motion I had Ris off of me and on her back. I could hear one of whomever this "them" was inhale sharply as my ass arched up in the air and I licked and savored every inch of skin I could reach without going exactly where Ris wanted me to.

I sucked and teased every inch of her body from her neck to her toes, never going anywhere near her pussy. I let my fingers wander there, but I wouldn't slide them in. I'd run my lips and tongue around it but never across. The thought of Ris with *any* man gave me such a feeling of anger and rage. I wanted her to beg, but most importantly I wanted her to beg *me*. I parted her legs and pressed myself up against her. Our wetness intermingling, I gently ground my hips into her, not enough to give her what she wanted but just enough to make her want more. Ris closed her eyes and threw her head back, trying to press herself back into me but I wouldn't allow it. She moaned in frustration.

"Say it," I whispered, getting tired of playing this game with her. I twisted, grinding my clit into hers just a little harder this time. We both gasped at the sensation, but I wasn't giving in. Still she refused. I got back on my knees and licked my way down her stomach. I circled her clit with my tongue and smiled to myself when her legs started to shake. I'd get her right to the edge and then . . .

"Okay, please. Now. Michelle, I'm sorry."

I had no idea what the hell she meant about being sorry until it hit me. And I mean it really did hit me. Before I could figure out what was going on I was damn near about to explode. He hit me with long deep strokes, grabbing me roughly by the back of my neck and pressing my face down into Ris so I could continue to savor her while I was being fucked hard from behind. I don't know how I did it, but I was able to concentrate just enough to get Ris back to the point where her legs were starting to shake and tighten around my face, her back arching off the bed. It was all sensory overload. The combination of wet pussy in my face and on my lips and the noises Ris was making only fueled the fire that Keyshawn was stroking up behind me.

One hand still had me by the back of my neck and the other had me by my ass, forcefully pulling me back into each stroke every time he drove forward. The sensations were driving me right over the edge. I couldn't fight it anymore. I pressed my lips hard against Ris's clit, knowing exactly how and where I'd send her. Right at that very moment Keyshawn drove one long, deep thrust that hit my "G, H, and damn I didn't even know that was a spot" and I went into my own free fall. I moaned, cried out, hell I'm pretty sure I spelled the nigga's name too as I fell forward—my legs, suddenly traitors to my body, no longer offered to support my weight. Waves of pleasure crashed over my body, so intense they were damn near painful.

I couldn't believe I'd turned down a lifetime of this feeling, a lifetime of dick downs, by marrying a woman. All I could do was lie there temporarily "dickmatized." That's when a nigga strokes it so good you suffer from temporary paralysis; all you can do is lie there para- lyzed. The room could have burst into flames and the devil himself could've jumped out at my ass and it wouldn't have gotten me up off that bed. Ris was stiff beneath me, still breathing heavy. I lifted my head long enough to offer her a weak smile before letting my face sink back into the warm softness of her stomach.

"Guess I did a damn good job huh?"

Okay, scratch everything I said before. If it weren't for the fact that my legs felt like Jell-O, I definitely would've jumped completely the fuck off the damn bed, ninja style. I looked back in complete and utter shock to see Lania crouching on her knees behind me. She was proudly stroking the head of her strap like it was a real dick. She smiled smugly at my expression. I looked down at Larissa, confusion written all over my face.

"Ris, what the fuck?"

She gave me an awkward smile, wrapping her arms around my neck and pulling me up toward her into an even more awkward hug.

"I'm sorry baby, I kind of lost a damn bet. But I figured, what da hell, you'd enjoy a li'l threesome."

"Shit, I definitely enjoyed the show."

My head swiveled toward Keyshawn and Curtis, who were sitting over on a sofa in front of the TV. The back of the sofa faced the bed so now it made sense why I didn't see them before. Keyshawn's head was tilted slightly and he wasn't smiling or looking anything close to his usual self. I hoped I hadn't embarrassed him by calling out his name. I just chalked up the way he was acting to the fact that he was probably ready to go stroke one out right quick, if he hadn't already.

"But, Lania, I saw you, I . . . I thought they were takin' you to a hospital?" *What the hell kind of game is this? Is this some sort of bullshit swingers dinner party?*

"Oh, that? It was nothing, just too many shots early in the day and really good coke. It happens. I'm fine as you can see."

Somewhere an alarm was going off. Realizing it was my phone, a special ringtone I'd set for Jim, a sudden chill came over me as all the blood seemed to drain from my body.

"Oh God, where are my clothes? That's my phone where is it?" I crawled off the bed in a panic, my legs still wobbly and my head pounding. I found my phone and pressed answer.

"Michelle, it's Jim. There's been an incident at the house. The children are fine and I'm on my way there now. I don't want you to be too alarmed but someone tried to break in and we're holdin' 'til you get here. Ain't callin' no cops yet. Gonna let you talk to 'em first."

"Oh God, are you sure the kids are okay? Is it Rasheed?"

"Rasheed?" Larissa sat up in the bed with the comforter pulled up to her chest.

I cursed to myself. I'd forgotten about keeping her out of the loop. Oh well it was too late; so much for that plan.

"What da fuck you mean? Is who Rasheed, Michelle?"

There was entirely too much going on with Jim trying to give me details and Ris on the verge of a spastic panic attack.

"Jim, I'm on my way. Larissa, just put your shit on, we have to go *now*. I'll explain in the damn car."

I could see the questioning looks on both Key's and Lania's faces but I ain't have time to explain. Shit, after what just went down we were way past the formalities stage. They'd just have to fuckin' understand. My hands were shaking so bad I could barely put my clothes on and bright spots kept flashing before my eyes. I'd bet everything on the fact that Rah wouldn't try to go after my kids and I was dead-ass wrong. *What kind of monster had prison turned him into that he'd try to hurt his own children?*

CHAPTER 13

BLOOD MOON . . . BLOODY MONEY

"So when exactly was you gonna tell me you knew for sure Rah was back?" Ris didn't wait five seconds for the limo to start moving before she started in with the questions.

"Damn, Larissa, I just found out my damn self."

"You ain't think I needed to know dat shit? What was you tryin'a do, make friends wit' his ass or somethin' before you told me?"

I was not in the mood. I just wanted to hold my babies, make sure they were okay, and get past this new chapter of bullshit as quickly as possible.

"Look, I handled the shit okay? What the fuck good would it have done if I did tell you, aside from have your ass worried too?" I'd started grinding my teeth so hard my jaw hurt. I stared out the window, content with watching what little traffic there was on the road at 4:00 A.M. whiz by, anything to keep me calm until we got to the house, anything to keep Ris from bringing up all of her insecure-ass doubts about Rasheed. I let my eyes wander and focus on the moon glowing a bright reddish orange in the distance. It was so big it looked like I could reach right out and touch it.

"Do you miss him? I mean y'all was togetha for a long-ass time. Ain't nothin' wrong wit' missin' the nigga."

She was pushing my damn buttons.

"If I was wit' a nigga for that long, I'd pro'ly miss his ass. Even after bein' wi'chu all this time. I can't even lie. But unlike how you do me I probably wouldn't lie to yo' ass 'bout it, Michelle."

"How many times do I have to tell you I don't miss that nigga? Stop fuckin' askin' me. Stop bringin' it up. Just fuckin' stop! And why you ain't tell me Keyshawn came by the damn house?" I was so pissed my voice cracked.

"He just came by to bring me my autographed ball. Said you weren't answerin' his calls. Why you gettin' so mad if you ain't got nothin' to be mad for?"

Her question made absolutely no fucking sense. I didn't know where it came from but it was there. I felt outright rage. Maybe it was because I was under too much stress, I wasn't sure. My hand went across Ris's face so fast her head snapped to the side and still it didn't feel like enough. All the shit I did for her, everything I bought for her, everything I did, I did to make her ass happy and I didn't get anything in return for it but bullshit.

My entire world revolved around Larissa and the kids and making sure they had everything they needed. Suddenly it was all too much for me. Ris was staring at me, holding her cheek, disbelief written all over her face at the fact that I'd even dared to hit her. In that moment I didn't see her as a wife, or a partner, lover, or a friend. She was a possession. I clothed, fed, watered, provided, and she'd take, took, and keep taking.

My rationale was nothing like anything I'd ever thought of before but the fact that she'd dare to question me relentlessly and challenge me and then tonight she would be so bold as to offer *my body* to another *woman* as consolation for a bet *she lost!* Growling like a mad woman I lunged across the limo. There was nothing that I wanted more in that single moment than to just choke the living fuck out of her dumb ass.

"Michelle, what da fuck is wrong wi'chu?" she shrieked, drawing her knees into her chest. Larissa kicked at me but I just grabbed her legs, digging my fingers into her thighs, purposefully bruising her, trying to hurt her.

"Whoa now! There's no need fer all that."

I was grabbed by my shoulders and pulled backward out of the limo. I was so caught up in my anger I hadn't even noticed that we'd stopped. I gave Larissa one last glare before straightening myself up and turning to Jim. Damn I was gettin' out of shape. It took me a few deep breaths before I could speak.

"Sorry about that, Jim. Please tell me what's going on."

He looked shyly toward Ris, who was now starting to climb out of the car. Her hair was a bird's nest on top of her head and I'd torn her fishnet top and broken one of her heels. I was so glad Jim already knew who she was, because I'd hate trying to explain why I was but really wasn't just trying to beat a stripper's or a call girl's ass in my limo.

"Well, like I said on the phone I didn't want to alarm ya. Jackson, over there, works for the Miami PD. He's already started the forensics so we won't have any issues."

"Wait, forensics? I thought you said the kids were fine." *No, I know I heard him say that there was nothing wrong with my babies. I know I wasn't that damn out of it when we talked.* I was shaking my head back and forth, my eyes filling with tears and my heart splitting in half because I was already thinking the words that no mother wants to hear.

"Right. Right. The kids were taken to get somethin' to eat. We had to get 'em away from here. Didn't want 'em seein' too much more than they might already have."

Jim needed to hurry the fuck up and explain to me what was going on, because if he hadn't noticed I was in an ass-whooping mood, and not only did I not see my babies but I had no clue where Rasheed was at or if he was dead or alive.

"Okay, Jim, I need the CliffsNotes version. I can't take this long, drawn-out shit."

"Ahhh, well. Blood on the moon tonight. Reckon we should have known somethin' would be afoot some-where. Darla was stabbed in the livin' room on the couch. We have her over there in the truck if you'd like to see her." He started to walk toward the truck and Ris and I followed him. Hearing that Darla didn't make it and knowing it could have been me or Ris made me im-mediately regret how I'd treated her on the ride home. I put my arm around her in an attempt to comfort her.

"I'm so sorry I got that mad at you," I whispered to her as we followed Jim. It suddenly dawned on me that the "her" he was referring to wasn't Darla. There was someone sitting in the back of one of the cars Jim approached. I recognized Keith from the highway and exchanged a polite smile with him.

"See now from what we can tell, she swam in from the ocean and climbed up to that third-story window that was left open 'round back. Keith was the first one inside after hearin' Darla scream, an' apprehended her. The li'l ones were asleep, didn't see it happen." Jim swung open the driver's side door and the interior light beamed on. Ris and I both stared at the younger black woman in the back seat but neither one of us recog-nized her. I shook my head at Jim.

"She ain't got no ID. Won't talk either. I was hoping maybe y'all would know who she might be."

I stared harder at the girl in the back of the car. Rah was good for conning young women; that's what he did for a living at the strip club. He conned women out of their bodies, their youth, their money, and eventually their minds. She couldn't have been any older than nineteen, maybe twenty, very slender and dark skinned, her hair cut into a edgy, curly Mohawk; nothing like the princess-dancer types Rah messed with back home. She refused to make eye contact with any of us, content with staring down at the floor in the car. I didn't place her face and couldn't figure out how or when I would have ever run into her in Florida or Virginia. I'd turned to walk toward Jackson, who was now calling the scene into the police, when I heard a whisper.

"Blood for blood money."

"What ye' say there, young lady?" Jim approached her, his head tilted to the side.

I didn't need her to repeat it. I'd heard her loud and clear and I knew exactly what it meant, but this was so unlike Rah to send a woman to do his dirty work. There had to be a reason why he wouldn't have come himself.

"Jim, where exactly did you send my kids?"

"Just down the street with David and Jacob. There was a little twenty-four-hour diner where they could get pancakes an' cocoa while we cleaned up and got the nanny's body outta the house."

Panic was coursing through my system. *Did Rasheed send that girl here as a decoy? Was she supposed to distract us, or do something to flush us out on purpose so he could get to the kids?* I didn't think anymore, I just took off running.

"Baby? Where you goin'?"

I didn't answer Ris. There wasn't any time. I'd explain after I had my kids in my arms. Until I saw that they were okay there was no room for anything else.

My car was blocked in on one side of the driveway by Jim and the other guys' vehicles. I ran into the house and grabbed Ris's car keys from the ring beside the front door. I didn't dare look into the living room. I was too scared to see Darla and all the blood. I ran out into the garage and climbed into the red convertible. It was the only car on the side of the garage that I could get out so the kids would just have to sit in each other's laps when I picked them up. I'd risk a ticket, fuck it.

I pressed the garage door opener and sped out. Jim and Ris both called after me but I didn't stop. I had to get to Trey and Lataya before Rasheed did, or at least if he was already there maybe, just maybe, I could talk him out of whatever he was planning on doing. The diner Jim mentioned was no more than a few blocks away and the sun was just starting to come up, illuminating the layer of dust on Ris's car. I made a note to get all of the cars washed later.

I could see the sign for the diner and signaled, braking to turn into the parking lot. The kids were coming out with two big guys on either side of them. They looked fine, smiling and laughing, and I smiled for the briefest moment before realizing that the digital gauge on the Benz was accelerating on its own. I stomped the brake pedal with everything I had but the car kept speeding up.

The sun was back in my eyes again and I pulled down the visor. That's when I noticed the slender, small, feminine handprint in the dust on the hood and I realized what that girl was doing in our house. She hadn't come for the kids. Darla must have seen her, or caught her off guard when she was trying to get out of the house. I threw up the parking brake.

"Shit." It didn't do a damn thing. *She must have disengaged it.*

Fortunately it was early enough that there were barely any cars on the road on a Saturday morning and I was praying like I'd never prayed before as the car hit eighty, eighty-five, and ninety. I could see Jim's men in the rearview speeding to catch up with me. My heart felt like a runaway train in my chest; it was thudding so painfully I could barely breathe. At 145 miles per hour I could barely keep the car on the road, and I was coming to an area where I knew I wasn't going to make it. The turn was too sharp and I was going too fast to jump out.

Squeezing my eyes shut as tightly as possible I turned the steering wheel, praying that maybe, just maybe, I could Tokyo drift or do some kind of donut and keep-it-moving shit I'd seen in movies. For that split second the only sound I heard was my breath as I inhaled what I thought would be my last one. Piña colada air freshener and new car leather would be the last smells I'd ever smell. The tires screamed and the best way to describe the body-jarring effects of slamming into a concrete wall is that it sounded and felt like God Himself put His foot down in the form of an underpass and I'd run right into it. Glass shattered as the passenger side crumpled, the car frame bending around me like a tin can tomb.

My life didn't flash before my eyes. I didn't relive all my happiest moments. In the blink of an eye I went from scared shitless to pitch black.

CHAPTER 14

I SAID—LOVE IS A HELLUVA DRUG

"Michelle? Try to squeeze my finger if you can hear me."

Ugh. Who is this squawking-ass woman in my ear? My head was killing me and my mouth felt like straight yuck. Like I hadn't brushed my teeth or drunk anything since who knew when. I felt so tired. I didn't even bother trying to open my eyes. All I wanted to do was drift back into the dark silence that I'd somehow slipped out of.

"I need you to squeeze, Michelle."

"Scream." My voice sounded crackly and froggish to my own ears. I could barely speak above a groggy, funky whisper. I tried and, damn it, I couldn't squeeze shit. But if she didn't shut the fuck up . . .

"What? Say it again. Use your words, Michelle. Say it to us again."

Oh my God, I groaned to myself, *will she ever stop?* I just wanted some ice water and lots of sleep.

"Shut. Fuck. Up. Scream." It took all the energy I had to get those words out, but whoever the fuck she was left me no choice; she'd refused to let up.

"Well, you are definitely a gutsy one. I think everything will be just fine, Larissa. You can come and talk to her if you'd like; she can definitely hear you."

"Hey, Chelle."

God, if I weren't so tired . . . I tried to say "hey" back to my baby but I was just so damn weak. It felt like the life had somehow been drained out of me and all I was left with was this darkness. Ris sounded so pitiful. I could her sniffling and blowing her nose, and all I could recall was me hitting her and being so nasty to her.

"I love you so much, bae, an' I hope you can forgive me."

I didn't know what I was supposed to forgive her for when I was the one who acted like a complete fool, hittin' her and shit. Maybe she just meant she was sorry for her being an all-around bitch for the last few weeks. I smiled in my mind and let myself drift back into that quiet, dark place, praying that Bird Bitch wouldn't come back for at least a few hours so I could get some rest.

When I'd finally come to my senses I found out I was in Memorial Hospital. The car wreck put me in a coma for a week and I slept off and on for a good week afterward. Ris and the kids came to see me every day and I could remember vague bits and pieces of hearing Trey's or Lataya's little voices saying they loved me or asking me to wake up. Ris said tears would roll down my face when the kids would talk to me but aside from that I was pretty much unresponsive. I even thought I'd heard Keyshawn's voice a few times, but I could have been dreaming. Thankfully, even though the car was totaled, I didn't suffer any serious injuries. Still, no one could believe I'd survived the crash. They'd been doing all types of blood work and screenings, trying to make sure I was at 100 percent and clear to be released, when Dr. Traverson came in. As soon as she spoke I immediately knew who she was.

"Michelle, I'd like to ask you a few questions." She glanced at Ris. "Alone please."

I nodded for Ris to wait outside so Bird Bitch and I could have this private convo.

"Okay, what seems to be the problem?"

"The toxicology reports came back from the lab. Now, initially we asked you several times, upon waking, if you were a user of any types of recreational substances, legal or illegal."

I stared blankly at her, waiting for further explanation, not completely understanding where this was going. "I don't use drugs, Dr. Traverson. Never have. I did leave a party and did have a few drinks. I told you that, and my wife told you that also." I was now frowning at her, confused as to why she would insist on asking me these same questions damn all over again.

"I understand your dilemma. You have young children in a same-sex household. A drug-related automobile accident and investigation would not bode well for you or your children, I'm sure."

"What the fuck does my sexuality or how I raise my children have to do with any of this? I don't use drugs. Someone did something to my Benz. I was almost murdered and you have the nerve to come after me? Jim Bartell can vouch for all of this, any mechanic can look at my car and tell you it was tampered with." My head was starting to pound and the IV in my hand was itching, aggravating me. For a second, I debated on snatching the thing out of my skin and just marching my ass right out of that damn hospital.

"The toxicology report shows you had pretty high levels of cocaine and ketamine in your system, Michelle. We kept you sedated initially as a means of rehabilitation, to ease the withdrawal symptoms. Would you like to tell me, on average, about how often you use?" She waited and I stared at her like she was a complete idiot.

"Michelle, we have several very highly recommended and very confidential programs I'd like to recommend to keep you from relapsing once we release you."

"Oh hell no, there has got to be some kind of mix up. I . . . I barely touch a glass of wine here and there but I would never do that kind of shit to my body. What the hell is ketamine?"

The thought of possibly losing my children over some dumb shit like this was making me want to slide right back into another damn coma. *What the fuck really happened at that party with Keyshawn?* I tried to remember every single little detail because that was the absolute last time I could remember even being under the same roof as any kind of drugs. My body shook uncontrollably as tears fell down my face. My life was falling apart and there seemed to be nothing I could do to pull it back together.

"Dr. Traverson? I'm sorry, did you say we was gonna lose our kids?" Ris had poked her head into the room. She'd obviously been listening the entire time.

I lay back and rolled onto my side on the hospital bed facing the wall. For the moment, I was content with just hugging myself and crying quietly. I didn't care to look at Ris or Bird Bitch right that second.

"Yes, Larissa, it is possible. If the mother has an ongoing issue with a controlled substance and refuses assistance, I may have to suggest that we get the state involved before we can release her back into the household. She was in a life-threatening accident under the influence and next time the children could very well be in it with her. It is highly possible that the children will be taken into Child Protective Services. Doctor-patient confidentiality prevents me from discussing this any further with you, however."

Fuck that shit, I'll just get myself a damn good law-yer. These types of things get fought all the time and won. I just ignored Bird Bitch.

"Well, Dr. Traverson, um . . . what if she ain' know she was um . . . actually doin' cocaine or anything else? I mean like voluntarily?"

That one simple little question made all the blood rush to my head. The vein in my forehead suddenly throbbed and probably swelled to the point that I looked like Frankenstein.

"And how on earth would she *not know* she was consuming an illegal narcotic, Larissa? Several *illegal* narcotics?"

I couldn't move, suddenly thinking, *Yeah, Larissa, how the fuck would I not know?* I was scared that if I made eye contact with her the look on my face would suck the life from her body, killing her on the spot and the truth would never be known. Then I'd still be right here, stuck in the same dumb-ass situation. So I didn't dare move a single, solitary muscle or make a sound.

"Um, it . . . it wasn't meant to be like for her to have no habit or nothin'. I jus' did it 'cause I read somethin' in this book we have in our library. You see, there was this voodoo priestess and she wanted her chieftain to come to her bed every night and not sleep with his other wives or ho around. *So,* every day she gave him a slow-acting poison and every time he chose her for sex she'd give him the antidote."

I was pretty sure Bird Bitch and I had the same exact "bitch, is you crazy?" look on our faces while Ris was talking.

"Well what happened is, eventually the chieftain got rid of all the other women and picked priestess 'cause he realized he always felt the best when he was with her and only her."

She paused, taking a deep breath the same way Trey did whenever I caught him in a lie and he was forced to tell me the truth; the rest of her words came out in rushed detail.

"So I got some coke—not no street shit. They cut that wit' who knows what and that could fuck somebody up somethin' serious and I ain't want that to happen. I put it on my finger and stuck it in her ass one day durin' sex. She ain't even like that shit, Doctor, and I swear she ain't know. I jus' figured if she got a high from sex wit' me she wouldn't want anyone but me, an' the only way I could give her the coke without her knowin' was anally—so that might be why she tested positive, 'cause it was pharmaceutical grade. I mean like really good shit." Larissa had started crying by the end of her fucking confession and I was two seconds away from tryin' to figure out if I could press charges on some shit like that or just whoop her ass. I still couldn't believe this shit.

"You did what to me?! All that li'l 'lemme show you a trick, play wit' ya ass' bullshit? Ris! My ass was numb for like two days! Did Lania have it on her strap too? Did y'all give me anything that night?"

Ris shrugged and I immediately regretted my outburst, lying back down, out of breath, my head feeling like it was splitting in half. I couldn't believe it. I was just flabber-fuckin'-gasted at this one. Bird Bitch was standing there, shaking her head back and forth in disbelief with her mouth opening and closing. She obviously wasn't used to lesbian sex, foreplay, or any of the toys, and we'd just given her a crash course.

"I . . . I . . . I'll l . . . leave you t . . . two alone for a m . . . moment." She spun her tight-faced self around and marched out of the room so fast I was surprised the tiles didn't fly up off the damn floor.

There was nothing for me to say to Ris. All I could do was lie there staring at her in utter disbelief. She stood there crying, looking back at me like a damned fool. *Voodoo priestess?* Those were old wives' tales, folklores. Out of all the life-empowering shit I had up in the library I just couldn't believe she'd actually read that particular one and tried to actually apply that shit to our life. What if I'd gotten addicted, or she'd gotten hold of some bad "pharmaceutical" shit and it'd killed me?

"I only did it—"

Holding up my hand I turned my face away, unable to look at her any longer. I didn't even want to hear it. I'd been drugged by my own wife. Never in a million years.

"Baby, I don't wanna lose you. I love you."

I ignored her. On one hand I had my ex trying to kill me, and on the other hand, my wife drugging me to keep me. *What the fuck kind of bullshit karma is this?* I just couldn't seem to catch a damn break.

CHAPTER 15

KARMA'S A BITCH . . . ONLY IF YOU ARE

They finally said I could be released after being stuck in that hospital for damn near two and a half weeks. Honestly, I thought Bird Bitch was just scared that me or Ris was gonna try to take her damn cookies when no one was looking. You know, since Ris rolled up in there and had her thinking we were lesbo, coke-sniffing, playing-in-ya-booty swingers. Wasn't nobody worried about Bird Bitch's old scary ass, I just wanted to go home. I'd asked Jim to arrange for a car to pick me up. I didn't want Ris driving me anywhere and definitely not in one of our cars until I could have them checked out. I guessed Rasheed thought he'd actually killed me or something, because the entire time I'd been in the hospital everything seemed to be pretty quiet.

"Michelle you *have* to use the wheelchair; it's policy."

I glared at Bird Bitch, happy that this was the last order and hopefully, the last time I'd ever have to hear her annoying-ass high-pitched voice. Reluctantly, I sat down and let the orderly wheel me to my car. Covering my eyes with my hand, I was momentarily blinded by the sudden exposure to the midday July sun. As the automatic door opened I welcomed the transition from hospital air to real air as it rushed over me. I waited for my eyes to adjust. I was literally thawing out. The transition from the cold, sterile hospital to the humidity and the sun on my skin made me feel alive again. Ris had brought my favorite turquoise sundress and flip-flops for me to wear home and I was thankful because any more clothing and I'd be sweating my ass off.

Walking into the house I couldn't help feeling a mixture of remorse and happiness. The place was just as I'd left it. Except for some ugly-ass oversized cream and tan couch where my old dark chocolate leather one used to be. *That shit better be stain guarded. Ris must've picked it out because there is no way I want the kids jumping they li'l asses all over a cream couch.* I frowned, the memory of why I needed a new couch suddenly making me feel sick to my stomach.

"Mommeeeeee." Trey ran up to me and I kneeled down and squeezed him so hard he squeaked. I loosened up, kissing his little cheeks. He smelled just like all little boys should smell—like cookies and dirt.

"You smell like a puppy," I teased him, rubbing my nose up against his neck, tickling him.

"I'm not a puppy. I'm a boy. Mommy an' me an' Taya have surprises for you."

The last person I really wanted to see was Ris, but I couldn't avoid her forever. "Okay, baby, where are they at?"

"Um I'm s'posed to keep you occ . . . occ . . ."

I smiled at his little scrunched-up forehead, deciding to help him out with the word before he developed a stutter. "Occupied, baby?"

"Yeah"—he was nodding his head like I'd solved a riddle—"dat's da word him used."

"*That's* the word *he* used. And, who is this 'he,' baby?"

" Count know. Mommy said call him Daddy, but I didn't 'cause I wanted to ask you if he's Daddy, but Taya . . . Taya tried ta say it an' she said 'Da Da Da Da.'"

Lord, where the fuck is Ris at? What did Trey mean she told him to call somebody Daddy? I scooped Trey up, grabbed my cell, and marched toward the kitchen, confident that at any second I could have any one of my guys in there if I needed help. Hell, I done seen 101 movies where the psycho killer takes the whole family hostage and all kinds of crazy shit happens so I was ready for damn near anything. I guessed it was time to face the music and deal with this nigga face to fuckin' face. Man to woman.

"Trey, man, what happened to keepin' her occupied?"

"I'm only four." Trey shrugged in my arms. "Nex' time jus' lemme watch da cookies."

I couldn't believe who was standing in front of the oven with my favorite pink apron tied around his waist and pink oven mitt on one hand. He was trying to balance Lataya on one hip and pull the cookies out the oven with the other. Keyshawn looked awkward as hell, and right at home in my kitchen.

He was wearing a fitted black tank top and plaid tan and black shorts with some Perry Ellis boat shoes. *Damn.* Now this was a nice welcome home present. Looking around I didn't see Ris anywhere; agitation immediately set in. *She could've at least been here when my ass walked up in the house.* I put Trey down.

"Baby, go play in your room. I'll bring you some cookies as soon as they cool down."

Lataya was already asleep and once she was out, she was out. I peeled her out of Key's arm. My hand slightly brushed Key's skin and sparks shot through my body from the contact. The man looked like he was made out of solid muscle. I took Lataya and put her on the couch in the living room.

"So um, what are you doin' here and where's Ris?"

"Larissa told Lania 'bout the accident and shit. We both offered to help out. Lania jus' took her to get you a welcome home present so I volunteered to watch the kids. She thought you'd be home later than this."

I was scared to ask Key what exactly Ris had told him. Couldn't have been but so much or anywhere near the truth since the nigga was standing in the middle of my kitchen in a pink apron baking cookies. He pulled off the mitt, proudly examining his handy work. Smiling up at him I couldn't help teasing. "Well now, it's nice to see those hands are good for somethin' other than handlin' a damn basketball and jugglin' women, Betty Crocker." He gave me a mischievous grin back and I felt something I hadn't felt in years: butterflies.

"Oh no, they can handle plenty more than that and the women. They just keep me busy until the right one settles me down."

Somehow one of those cookies seemed to magically float its way up to my lips. Okay, the nigga fed me the cookie. But it was *the way* he did it. Once again I found myself as the focal point of his almond-shaped brown eyes. We were so close I could see that his lashes were short, thick, and extremely curly. I was just as mesmerized with him as he seemed to be with me. I could feel my heart starting to speed up; just being close to this man made my body follow its own agenda, no matter what my mind told it.

"So it seems as though we're both in completely unsatisfying situations. I think maybe we should join forces. Work on satisfying a few things."

That fool could've said "let's go sit and translate Latin in a library" for all I know and my ass still would've said "okay."

Warmth brushed up against my bottom lip and instinctively they parted. It could've been the fact that I'd been eating hospital food for the last couple of weeks but I couldn't help this shit, I had a straight-up big girl moment. Closing my eyes I moaned. This nigga made the *perfect* chocolate chip cookie. *Oh my God.* Ain't nothin' in this world like a cookin' or bakin' muthafucka. I lie to you not.

"My turn." I smiled, breaking one of the cookies in half, raising it up to Key's full pink lips.

He went in for his bite, and stepping in closer I moved ever so slightly, denying him his treat and leaving a trail of warm chocolate across his lower lip. He inhaled sharply, surprised when I leaned up on my toes and softly licked and sucked on his bottom lip until all the chocolate was completely gone.

"Mmmm." He raised an eyebrow, licking his lips. The action sent a wave of sexual awareness through my body. "I guess I get anotha turn since Michelle switchin' up the rules."

He was running his finger along the curve of my chin, toward my ear, down to my collarbone.

"Who the hell said we had rules?" I sounded like I'd just finished hiking up the side of Mount Everest.

He smiled at my comment before pulling me into a deep, long kiss that set my blood on fire and awakened the ocean in between my legs. It took my breath away and damn near made my knees give out at the same time. My eyes flew open and I gasped at the sudden warmth against my neck. *No, this nigga didn't.* But the light dusting of crumbs across my chest and all over the floor confirmed he'd just crushed that mu'fucka all over the side of my neck. He smiled against my lips before lowering his head, drifting his tongue lazily across my skin, treating the chocolate on my neck the same way I'd treated the chocolate on his lips. He stopped just long enough to lift me onto the counter beside the stove.

I untied my apron from around his waist and replaced it with my legs, my dress riding so far up my legs I could feel the cold counter against the back of my thighs. Sliding the straps to my dress down just past my shoulders, I took another cookie from the tray and stuck my finger into one of the gooey chocolate chips. I watched Key seductively as he watched me smear chocolate down the middle of my neck and even lower around my half-exposed nipple. He was rock solid; I could feel it through the barrier of his shorts pressed between my legs bulging up against me, the heat searing through my thin cotton panties. My thighs flexed involuntarily. He didn't need any more urging than that before lowering his head and pulling my chocolate-covered Hershey's Kiss nipple into the heat of his mouth, sucking hard.

Ripples of pleasure started at my hair follicles, and shot all the way down to my toes and back up again. Instinctively, I ran my hands underneath his tank top; he felt like warm marble covered in skin. His lips were working their magic on my nipples, left then right. Yes, he was definitely earning these milk and cookies. The top of my sundress had fallen almost down to my waist and I bit my lower lip hard when Key cupped my breast together with one hand and licked both nipples at the same damn time. We both moaned when my hand slid down into the waistband of his shorts, and all I can say is, feeling is definitely believing.

My hand closed around as much of him as it could. I twisted my wrist and gently stroked him upward; he took a sharp, quick breath. Like riding a bike, I started to remember how empowering it felt to be able to weaken a man with one hand. He was thick, thicker than I remembered him looking, and all of a sudden I needed something else wrapped all around that mu'fucka. As if he'd read my thoughts Key reached down and lowered his zipper, freeing himself through the hole in his boxers.

We didn't waste any more time. Our eyes connected for the briefest moment before he kissed me hard. The heat from his fingers grazed my inner thigh as he slid my soaked panties to the side, pulling me forward on the counter. He buried himself as deep as he could go in one fluid stroke.

My ass had completely forgotten what the fuck a real dick should feel like. I could feel every bit of me stretching around every single inch of him and it was a painfully pleasurable glimpse of heaven.

Breaking our kiss, I buried my face into his neck, biting into his skin to keep from moaning or screaming out loud. My nails had to be hurting him; I was digging them in like I was a rock climber and his back was the damn mountain. Every stroke sent a shockwave of pleasure through my body like one of those sonar pulses they use to ping the ocean.

"Damn, Michelle, you gonna have me all marked up. I got appearances to make, baby."

I kissed his skin, offering him a silent apology. "I wanna scream so bad, baby. I can't help it." My reply was no more than a breathless whisper against the side of his neck. I would've promised that I wouldn't do it again but I was used to being rough and being handled just as roughly in return. There was something about finding a bruise or a mark the next day that always made me smile secretively at the fun I had earning my "battle scars."

"Don't worry 'bout it, baby, daddy'll fix it."

My eyes drifted closed. I felt weightless. The nigga didn't miss a beat. He slid me off the counter and held me up against him. I tightened my legs around his hips and wrapped my arms around his neck. The excitement, the thrill of being caught, all of the above just acted as fuel to the powder keg about to explode inside my pussy, and this mu'fucka's dick was the damn fuse.

He palmed my ass in each hand, the heat from his long fingers searing my skin as he guided my pussy up and down the length of him. My head fell back, a soft moan leaving my lips. Fuck, he was about to get bit again and he must've sensed it coming because before I could even close my mouth or get anywhere near his neck, it was full of cookie. I glared at him, an angry frown creasing my forehead, and then I completely forgot why I was frowning in the first place. Mouth full of damn chocolate chip cookie, I chewed on that to keep from chewin' on him.

"Chelle, this shit so good," he moaned quietly in my ear, wrapping his arm around my body tightly he started to stroke deeper and harder.

I could feel every vein, every throb, my muscles contracted and the walls closed in around him. It hit me like a wall of electricity that started in my pussy, working its way outwards to my fingertips and toes—my powder keg *exploded*. I couldn't breathe, couldn't hold myself up. Eyes closed, I let myself float on each wave as it came in.

Key quickly pulled out and I felt liquid heat hit the back of my thigh as he stroked himself, his chest heaving like he'd just got off the court. He waited a few seconds before he sat me down.

I straightened my dress, wet a paper towel, and wiped myself down before sliding my panties back in place while he fixed his shorts, or at least tried to. There was no hiding the wet spot I'd left on them, and no, I wasn't sorry, but thankfully his shirt was long enough to cover it. I looked at the mess we'd made out of the cookies and laughed. *Lord, I might never let my babies eat another chocolate chip cookie again.*

"I'll take that as a yes?" Keyshawn walked over and smiled at me, expectantly waiting for a reply.

My response was to place a gentle kiss on his waiting lips because, honestly, I couldn't even remember the damn question.

It was another hour or so before Ris got back with nothing more than a flower arrangement, something that I was pretty sure Lania had a hand in picking out. It was way over the top, with birds of paradise and other exotic flowers. Ris knew for a fact that I loved lilies; they're the most fragrant and last the longest. I gave her a polite thank you and set the arrangement on the dining room table. I still wasn't ready to deal with her. It didn't matter how many times she apologized or tried to explain her side of the situation. The bottom line was, I'd have never drugged Larissa or given someone else permission to have access to her body without her consent. And, after the mind-blowing fuck session I'd just had with Keyshawn, there was the nagging question of whether I even wanted to be with her anymore. The constant uphill struggle of dealing with her on a day-to-day basis, constantly proving my faithfulness, and accounting for ever minor detail of my life was finally starting to wear me down. Aside from saying "thank you," I didn't bother speaking to her again until long after Key and Lania had left.

"Why you tell Trey to call that nigga Daddy?"

She was walking out of the bathroom, getting ready for bed. She tripped over the area rug at the sound of my voice. *I must have caught her off guard.*

"Huh? You talkin' 'bout Keyshawn?"

I sneered at her silently. Who the fuck else she think I was talking about?

"Oh, I was just playing—it was a joke. Trey pro'ly misunderstood it."

I didn't even feel like getting into it with her. As bad as I wanted to yell, "You don't joke with a two-year-old and a four-year-old about something like that," I just rolled over facing the opposite wall so my back would be to her for the rest of the night. It was definitely time for me to make a change.

The next morning I'd decided to skip work and just spend the day with the kids. We went out to breakfast and I watched my little boy put away a whole stack of pancakes like a grown-ass man. Lataya sat on my lap crushing bacon in her chubby little fists; she was getting more of it on me than in her mouth but she was quiet so I let her be. Trey chattered up a storm. I hadn't realized how much he'd grown up. It was like I'd missed the last two and a half years walking around in a daze. Ever since the move I'd made the mistake of puttin' another woman before my own flesh and blood and the thought pulled at my heart.

"Mommy, can we play wif Unca Key today?" He was so excited about the possibility of being around Keyshawn, his eyes lit up and he could barely sit still giving me his biggest "Mommy, please" smile. As bad as I wanted to tell him no, I had to admit it to myself: *shit, Mommy kinda wanted to play with Uncle Key too.*

"Let me text Uncle Key and see if he can come outside, okay?"

Good morning, Cookie Monster. Trey wants to
know if you can come out and play?

I waited anxiously, worried that it was too early in
the morning to be texting him or too soon to be trying
to play house with this nigga. A few seconds later my
iPhone whistled.

Sure, leavin' the gym. Gonna shower. Wanna meet
me at my place?

"Well, sweetheart, it looks like we'll be hangin' with
Uncle Key for a little while today."

The smile on Trey's face melted my heart. I never
wanted to admit it but he needed a man's influence in
his life—even if it was just for a few hours.

CHAPTER 16

CRIMES OF PASSION

A week had passed and Michelle still hadn't said more than a few words to me since being released from the hospital. It was eating me up inside. I'd apologized, begged, cried, and even cursed at her for making me do the things I'd do sometimes and still she wouldn't even so much as look at my ass. I couldn't think of anything else. She was s'posed to be on bed rest but decided to carry her ass to work against the doctor's orders. She even went so far as to take the kids with her, like I couldn't be trusted with them or some dumb shit. I called to check on her and my heart sank when every call went straight to voice mail. She was still heated. I guessed I just needed to face it. We were done and she was probably out seeing whoever she needed to see to talk about "Ris did this" or "Ris won't do that."

I'd tried to get my cousin Shanice to give me advice on the situation but she took Michelle's side, sayin' what I'd done was definitely fucked up and she'd be amazed if we weren't filing for divorce by the end of the damn month. Depressed and feeling completely fuckin' hopeless I hit up the connect I'd gotten from Keyshawn the day he'd dropped off my autographed basketball.

"This Tink, who this?"

That's how she always answered. The first time I'd called her to get the coke that I'd used on Michelle I thought I had the wrong number, but this time I knew better.

"Hey, boo, it's Ris."

"Hey. What's up, pud, you out lookin' at that silver BMW eight series again?" She was asking if I wanted an eight ball of the *good shit.*

"You know it. You know anyone who got a brand new one?" I answered the exact same way Keyshawn had told me to do the first time.

Tink's boyfriend, or King as they called him on the street, was the biggest dealer and the main supplier of the best shit on the entire East Coast. King's shit was pharmaceutical grade, so pure it was damn near translucent just like fish scales. It wasn't nothin' like that white powdery shit I used to get back home. Key hooked me up with Tink because she was what he called good quality and low risk. She only sold shit outta her personal stash that King gave her to use and she was under the radar. I just liked dealing with her because she was cute and cool as hell.

"Oooh, girl, I got you. Ya girl Lania jus' hit me up too. Why don't we have us a girls' day and hang out. We can go for a test drive, gas and drinks all on me."

Shit. If she was saying what I thought she was saying I ain't have no problem getting twisted for free. *Fuck!* I almost slapped my forehead in frustration. I'd forgotten all about Michelle's fucking hired idiots sitting outside. Even though they'd signed confidentiality agreements, basically meaning they couldn't say shit about what I did long as I ain't kill nobody, there was still no way I would expose Tink like that. I needed to think of a way to get rid of they asses so I could go out and have some playtime. I texted Lania to see if she could come by the house and pick me up, maybe bring Keisha or someone with her.

It wasn't long before I was standing in the doorway, my eyes the size of ostrich eggs, while Lania and her girls came in. The March of Dimes was what I'd call that shit. I was in lesbian heaven and I was sure the security guys outside were using all they expensive equipment to take close-ups so they could jerk off in the damn car later. Lania cat-walked over giving me her weird hug and air-kiss thing before introducing me to everyone.

"Larissa, you already know Keisha. This is Mercedes, Havannah, Sierra, Isys, Marisol, and Katia. They all work for me just like you, sweetie."

It was like looking at six of Baskin-Robbin's thirty-one flavors. These bitches was each as exotic as they names sounded and all of them were on some straight-up model shit. I mean makeup, pumps, hair, booty shorts, and baby-doll dresses all on point.

"It's nice meetin' all of y'all," I responded shyly.

All of a sudden I felt like the ugly duckling and even though she was being a complete bitch, being sur-rounded by all these beautiful swans made me miss Michelle even more. In all honesty Michelle never made me feel anything less than beautiful when we were around other women, and I could have used a little of that right now. I swallowed past the damn lump that formed in my throat and started to look each girl over. Lania stood beside me doing the same.

"You and Havannah look almost identical minus the eye color. She is sure to be perfect."

I was shocked. Havannah was the smallest of all the women and the second most beautiful in my opinion, the first being Lania. She was shaped like a mermaid, full and thick hips, small waist, and big old titties. She had what I'd heard white folk refer to as classical beauty. High cheekbones and pouty lips with sleek cat-like dark brown eyes similar to Lania's. I immediately fell in love with her eyebrows. I wish my shits would arch perfectly the way hers did. The only major difference was that her hair was dyed a funky platinum blond and my hair was reddish brown. But after looking her up and down I had to agree with Lania's observation; it could actually work.

I stared out the tinted window of Lania's all-white Range waving at myself standing in the doorway, wet from a shower, wearing nothing but a blue silk robe, hair tied up in a towel. I removed my hat and started unpinning my hair once she was out of view. I was actually waving at Havannah's sexy ass pretending to be me. I'd put on her clothes, pinned my hair up underneath a sun hat, and when the March of Dimes sashayed they asses out the house I went right along with them.

In a few hours Havannah would throw on a pair of jeans and a T-shirt I'd left out for her, call herself a cab, and by the time everyone figured out what had actually happened I'd be on my way back to the house high and happy. Of course Michelle's ass was gonna be madder than a muthafucka when she found out, but fuck it. In my opinion, since she hadn't been speakin' to my ass all this time what difference would it make?

We stopped just long enough to drop the rest of the girls off at some restaurant before going to meet Tink. *I swear, every house I visit in Florida just gets bigger and more bad-ass than the last one.* My jaw damn near hit the floor when I saw the house King had Tink set up in. We rolled through what seemed like a never-ending stretch of bare beach and palm trees before finally pulling up to this beach-side mansion, and that muthafucka looked like it was made completely the fuck out of glass. I mean almost *every* single wall was on some complete floor-to-ceiling window type shit. How this bitch did anything during the day or at night with the lights on my ass didn't know, but the shit was fuckin' beautiful.

Tink breezed her way outside as we pulled up. Imagine my surprise when I first learned li'l Ms. Tink was a white girl, and pro'ly one of the nicest ones I'd ever met, too. She led us through her glass house, the scent of gardenia and honeysuckle following us wherever we went, like she'd washed the windows in some smell-goods. I was relieved when she took us into a room toward the back that overlooked the beach. My ass wasn't tryin'a sit up in somebody's living room doin' some illegal shit. Especially not with all these damn windows.

The room was painted in a mint green or sage on some straight-up Japanese zen type shit, and I loved it. There was a lava lamp in one corner on a tiny pedestal, and tall green bamboo plants grew along the window facing the beach, giving us a li'l privacy. In the middle of the room lavender and cinnamon-colored Japanese-style zafu and smile cushions sat around a small marble table. Yeah, my ass knew a little somethin'. Stuck up in the house all damn day watchin' HGTV and decorating shows, wishing I could swap out Michelle's old-fashioned *Masterpiece Theatre* furniture taught me a thing or two. We each picked a cushion and sat down while Tink pulled a silver box about the side of a shoebox from underneath the table and the party began.

We were on our third or fourth line and my head was already buzzing. My nose had gone numb and I was trying to figure out if I wanted to buy me some of that shit to take home.

"Who the fuck you got up in here, Tink?"

We all jumped when we heard his voice boom through the house.

"Damn, King, what I tell you 'bout comin' up in here, yellin' all up in my damn house?"

I wanted to laugh because Tink actually *yelled* back, but my heart was already flying because of the coke and now this heffa was mouthing off to a kingpin. Lord, we was gonna die.

He hovered in the doorway, his bark way more intimidating than his look. He couldn't have been taller than five foot eight, with not a lick of hair on his face. Put some money on it, I bet someone could rub Taya's ass with one hand, King's cheek with the other, and not know the damn difference. He looked like a damn kid to me. I couldn't tell if he was Italian or what; his dark olive complexion could easily go either way. He had wolf-lookin' crystal-clear grey eyes, focused on Lania. I was thinkin' maybe we was s'posed to get up and kiss the muthafucka's pinky ring or some shit. I ain't know.

"Angelo, how are you sweetie?" Lania smiled at him and got up to give him a way-too-friendly hug.

"Ahh, Lany, baby doll." His tone softened and all his Jersey-boy accent came through. "I been lookin' for you's. Tell dat brother of *your's* my people are telling me that shit is gettin' very real and that deadline is close."

I looked at Lania. *What the fuck—Lany?* was written all over my face. He had a nickname for her ass and everything. *What kinda shit is she up to?* I tried my best not to make my "oh shit" face. Hell, I ain't know what the fuck kinda expression I was makin'—I couldn't feel my damn face anymore. I started touching my cheeks and my eyebrows, trying to keep my face straight while also wonderin' why this King person looked kind of familiar.

And then it clicked. I remembered the party at Curtis's place. King was this fool's street name. Standin' in front of us was Angelo Testa, the billionaire. The one Keyshawn couldn't stand for whatever reason and now I guessed I knew why. Because the muthafucka was a straight-up dope dealer. *Ooooooh.* I tried to keep quiet while he and Lania continued their conversation.

"I've spoken to him several times. He's just more resilient than either of us, but to you we owe many thanks. Your advice has always weighed heavily on my brother's decisions."

I was getting nervous. It felt like just being in this bitch and leaving alive meant I would owe this muthafucka a favor or some shit. Fuck that, I wasn't about to be drug mulin' shit across state lines for his ass. I breathed a little easier when he nodded and walked off, but my ass was ready to get the fuck up outta there.

"Lania, I kinda wanna be home close to when Michelle gets off work an' it's already four-thirty. You almost ready?" I really didn't want to go home. I just didn't want to be around a damn drug boss. After watching Rasheed and everyone around him crumble, I knew too well how bad shit could go for these types of people no matter how good it seemed to be going. Besides, I thought this bitch was s'posed to be low-key; this shit wasn't no kinds of low-key.

"Um, Larissa, Keyshawn told me Michelle would be showing him a house at five-thirty today, so you can relax."

I looked at her fuzzy, high, confused.

"She wouldn't do that. She took the kids into the office wit' her this morning. You sure he meant today?"

"Shit, Key wouldn't lie to me. If he wants to fuck he can fuck. We are open, he has no reason to lie or hide anyone from me. I'll call him and ask." She whipped out her little Prada something custom phone, speed dialing his number.

Only because my ass was high as fuck, I laughed dead in her face when that shit went straight to voice mail. Tink was looking back and forth between the two of us weak at whatever this little drama was we had going on.

"Larissa, call your woman and see where she is." Tink was grinning, her face all lit up with excitement.

I looked at Tink and smirked. "My *woman* ain't answering my calls—hasn't been all damn day and knowin' her, she pro'ly' been laid up with Lania nigga havin' family time and shit."

My words were like the negatives to a photo and the picture was developing crystal clear up in Lania's head. She was suddenly blazing mad and I for once was the calm one. *Somebody give my ass a trophy,* I thought, crossing my arms to the cheers of the fake studio audience in my head. The only reason I was so calm was because I was used to sharing Michelle with another man. This type of bullshit came with the territory as far as dealing with her ass was concerned and I'd been doing it for years, but Lania was shaking she was so pissed off. I couldn't resist; I had to ask.

"Um, Lania, if I'm not mistaken, weren't you tryin' to get with Michelle?"

"Fuck no, I had a bet with Keyshawn I could fuck her first. Usually if I get them before him, it makes him not want them so much after."

Smart bitch. I had to give her ass credit for that little plan.

"But, Larissa, I'm telling you right now. I will *kill* your bitch wife if I get my hands on her."

Her threat didn't sit well with me, high or not; something made me believe she'd do it. I pulled out my phone and dialed Chelle's number, praying she'd pick up and be at the house or at her job. Once a-mutha-fuckin'-gain that shit went to voice mail and *now* my ass was getting mad and the crowd booed.

"Fuck this, we're going. Now." Lania jumped up and stormed out of the house, leaving me no choice but follow her ass or get left behind. *Damn, she could have at least let me ask for a doggie bag.* In my dulled state our convo played back in my head, Lania's words finally catching up with my brain, and the audience in my head yelled, *Hold the fuck up!*

"Wait. Did you say Chelle was showin' Key a house today? I thought he closed on his house already. Michelle told me that's why we were celebrating that first night at LIV." I had to damn near run to keep up with Lania's long-ass legs. The sand didn't even slow her ass down. The coke we'd done gave everything a pink halo in my mind. Like none of this shit was real. She still hadn't answered me as she hopped her ass up into her Range. I finally caught up and climbed in as well.

"Key hasn't bought any damn house. He still in his same damn house. What lies your bitch wife tell you? I'll cut out her tongue and feed it to her, before I kill her."

This time I didn't get mad at Lania; oh no, this time my ass was furious and it was with Michelle. I couldn't believe she'd lied to me! We sped down the highway to Keyshawn's *real* house. I was thinkin' high thoughts the whole way. I imagined Keyshawn fuckin' Michelle and remembered Lania fuckin' her with her strap. The kids calling Keyshawn Daddy, me sitting in a cell by myself. Blood on wood floors, all kinds'a crazy shit.

A part of me wanted her to be there so I could actually catch her in the act. That way she wouldn't be able to lie to me or convince me of no dumb shit. Another part of me wanted her and the kids to be home, or on their way home, so we could try to get shit back to normal as soon as possible.

Lania started to slow down and we pulled into the driveway of a large cream-colored house with a red shingle roof. It wasn't as big as all the other homes I'd been to. Not the kind of house I expected Keyshawn "Keys to the City" Matthews to have, but I guessed that's why he was tryin' to buy a new one in the first place.

"I don't see Michelle's car nowhere." I looked around a few more times, scared to let myself feel any kind of relief.

"It could be in the garage or around the back, or they could have gone down to the courts by the lake. We will see." Lania grabbed her purse and dumped everything out into the floor of the Range, M·A·C makeup and NARS shit going everywhere.

Man, this shit was fucking up my free high. Two high bitches doin' some dumb-ass high-ass shit. She took her empty purse and cat-walked even now around to a side. My TV audience chanted the *Pink Panther* theme music in my head. I tried to shake them out as I followed her to a side door.

"Lania, you got a key?" I whispered.

"He took it back last time we had an argument but"—bending down, she picked up a smooth, large, round garden stone—"I do now." Dropping it into her purse, she tapped it against the glass in the door, which shattered instantly. She threw the rock back into the bushes and used her purse like a glove to reach in and unlock the door.

"Nigga never turns his alarm on. No matter how many times I fuss and tell him about it, he never listens." She tsked, and we crept in, careful to step over the broken glass. We were in the kitchen and straight ahead I could see the living room. Luther Vandross's "Here and Now" was playing loudly throughout the house over the intercom speaker system. There were two empty wineglasses sitting on the kitchen table. Looking at Lania my eyes involuntarily filled with tears, and as much as my heart was hurting it broke me down even further to see hers do the same.

"Where would they put the kids?"

Michelle wouldn't fuck no nigga in front of Trey and Lataya; she wasn't that damn trifling. Lania's eyes widened and her finger flew over my lips, silencing me. I stared at her—confused, waiting. I physically watched her heart break and fall into a million pieces. I saw my own sad reflection in a single tear that slid down her cheek in slow motion and I heard the splash when it hit the floor. Yeah, I was that high.

"Oh my God this shit feel so good . . ."

My own eyes filled with tears. High as I was I didn't care anymore; I just wanted to confront Michelle, make her be sorry, and then I could take her back and we'd be even. Lania turned and set down her purse before we started walking toward the stairs and I followed closely behind her. Not used to the house, I was making sure I stepped where she stepped so I wouldn't trip over anything or make a floorboard creak. The carpet kept our steps quiet as we went through the living room.

I saw a couple of Legos scattered around and my knees almost gave out but I kept walking—past the large black circular-shaped couch and wall-sized flat-screen TV. Past a room that looked like it wasn't nothing but a shrine Keyshawn devoted to himself, full of trophies, and life-sized posters, until we came to the stairs. The house surround sound was playing Aaliyah's "At Your Best" and I thought I was gonna be sick

for a second. This was one of my and Michelle's songs
back in the day.

We got up to the top of the stairs and every *I love
you* replayed in my head, every kiss, every smile, every
happy memory, and all I could think about was seein'
her face so I could say, "Baby, I forgive you. Let's move
on." I almost turned around and went back down the
stairs, but we were right outside the bedroom door.
You could hear Keyshawn more clearly now. Lania just
stood there for a moment with her head down like she
was 'bout'a just die. I couldn't see her face but I could
tell by the way her shoulders were shaking, she was
crying hard—trying not to make a sound. I felt so sorry
for her. She turned the knob and I braced myself.

My eyes were ready for anything, Michelle naked
and on top or Michelle on her knees getting it from
the back, or, shit, Keyshawn on top and Michelle's
legs around his neck. I already started picturing it so it
wouldn't be as shocking when I finally got to see it. But
I don't think anything we ever picture in our heads actually prepares our asses for reality. The door opened
soundlessly and Aaliyah's voice sang the words directly
into my ears over the speakers: "You may not be in
the mood to learn what you think you know." It took
me longer to find them because I didn't know how the
damn room was set up or where the bed was. My high
ass scanned everywhere like I was FBI, taking every
little detail in at a glance. Pants, shirts, loafers all over,
soft light brown shag carpeting, blue candles lit on a
dresser. I could smell India Moon incense burning.

I stopped on the Trojan wrappers beside the foot of
the bed and when I finally saw them, I probably lost a
good five years off of my life based on the amount of
time that my heart stopped. I'm pretty sure I sprouted
'bout fifteen grey hairs, too. Before I could say anything

Lania was already across the room, and I tried, but I already knew I wouldn't be able to get to her fast enough. My TV audience screamed and I stood there, glued to the floor, watching everything in slow motion as she lunged at the bed, landing on top of the comforter. Landing right smack on top of Curtis's back.

"What the fuck, Yylannia? What the fuck you doin' in here?" Keyshawn jumped out the bed naked and, oooh, he was *maaaaad.*

I slowly backed my ass farther into the hallway just to make sure he ain't see me. Ain't want the nigga not hookin' my ass up at clubs an' shit anymore. *Boy oh boy, if Michelle only knew 'bout this shit.* Remember now, I said I scanned the room like the damn FBI! I ain't see no women's clothes or panties up in there and and I ain't neva' *hear* a woman, but Lania, aka Mrs. Muthafuckin' Action Jackson, was already in the room before I could point that shit out. But the circumstances still gave her a damn good reason to be goin' the fuck off the way she was.

Soundlessly, Lania climbed off of the bed. I waited to see what Curtis had to say but he didn't dare move. Embarrassed, I guessed. All I could do was shake my head at Mr. Big-time NBA Owner fucking his damn . . . Gasping, my hand flew to cover my mouth as a red stain began spreading across the light blue comforter. So much for trying to remain unseen; my sudden movement caught Keyshawn's attention. His eyes locked on mine. Full of anger and fear he started to walk toward me, but my attention went back to Lania, who was now looking down at the knife in her hand like she didn't even know she'd picked it up. Hell I didn't even know she'd picked it up.

"Well Mr. 'Keys to the City,' think they'll give you the keys to your cell?"

"*Noooo.*" Keyshawn's scream shocked me. My eyes widened 'cause I would've never pegged him as the screamin' type. Shit, I ain't see him as a bottom either but hey. He climbed onto the bed and grabbed Curtis's body, tryin' to stop the bleeding with his hands. Wiping the handle off with the comforter Lania laid the knife down. She smiled as she walked toward me, grabbed my hand, and we got the fuck from up outta there.

"Do you think he gonna call the police?" It was funny how we'd suddenly switched rolls and now I was frantic and on the brink of panic and Lania was calm as fuck.

"Who would believe him if he did? Someone broke in, took nothing, killed his gay lover who's also the owner of the team *and* left the murder weapon?"

We were now flying down South Dade Highway but in the opposite direction of home.

"Where are we going? I live the other way."

"To the beach for a little while. I know a shortcut so we can avoid traffic."

I checked my cell, disappointed that I only had one bar of battery power left and zero fuckin' missed calls. Well, for all the thinkin' I'd done about her ass earlier, if Michelle ain't miss me I sure as hell wasn't gonna miss her.

CHAPTER 17

STOP LOOKIN' AND LOVE WILL SOON LOOK BACK

It was around six-thirty when I was sitting in the photo booth at Chuck E. Cheese and my phone went off. It was Jim's ringtone and my heart immediately went into a downward spiral. *Lord give me strength for whatever this man had to tell me.*

"Hey, Michelle, got some not so good news."

I waited, wondering what the hell could have happened now. Me and the kids were fine so the only thing I could think was that something had happened to Ris. 1001 worst-case scenarios flashed before me and even though I hadn't figured out whether I was more mad at her actions or hurt by them, I instinctively began to worry.

"All right, Jim, I'm listening."

"Welp, the other missus done up an' gone AWOL on us."

My hands clammed up in a nervous sweat. *Ris had gone what?* The photo booth flashed pictures of the kids' smiling faces, and me looking like I was gonna wring someone's neck the second I stepped out of there. I adjusted the kids on my lap, holding the phone with my shoulder.

"What do you mean by AWOL, Jim? Does that mean you lost her? Why wasn't someone following her?

How'd they lose her? It's what the fuck I pay you guys for isn't it?"

Trey's eyes widened, giving me his "ooooooh, Mommy, that's a bad word" face, and I took a deep breath, trying to calm myself down. It wasn't working.

"Now, now. No need'n gettin' upset wit' my boys. They did what they was paid to do. She pulled a fifty-two switch up on 'em."

I started counting, but only made it to five before giving up. Rolling my eyes, I prepared myself for the bullshit. "CliffsNotes, Jim, quickly please, before I break somethin', an' what the hell is a fifty-two what-ever?" You would think he'd be used to telling me shit by now. Used to me wanting quick details an' short answers in *plain English.*

After a long, drawn-out sigh he explained, "A damn gaggle of 'em, all lookers, showed up 'round 'bout three o'clock an' went inside. Apparently Larissa swapped outfits wit' one of 'em, matched her size an' build to a T. Walked out on her own free will, right dab in the middle of the flock."

I swore I needed my own Jimtionary. It took me a moment to figure out what a gaggle and a flock had to do with any damn thing. I was out of the picture booth, cell phone on my shoulder, Lataya on my hip, and Trey dragging his damn feet, pouting beside me before Jim could even finish his explanation.

"Mommeeee, you forgot our pictur—"

I shot him that mother's shut-up-and-bring-yo'-ass-or-meet-certain-death look, stopping him dead ass in the middle of his whining. I'd definitely perfected that shit over the years.

"Keith said he recognized one of the young ladies. The driver was the one y'all like to associate wit', Yylan-nia. She was a part of the high jinks. The decoy, as we called her, caught a cab 'bout ten minutes ago an' that's when he noticed it wasn't Larissa. He went inside to look fer her, put two an' two together."

I tried to feel a little more at ease knowing that she was with Lania, but I knew Ris all too well. With everything that'd happened lately, this shit was her way of acting out. She was trying to do something she shouldn't be doing in order to cope with our shit and all the drama. Lania just so happened to be her enabler.

I buckled the kids into their car seats, upset that once again my babies had to take back burner to some more bullshit.

"Thank you, Jim. I'll call her and Keyshawn to see if he's seen them. I'm on my way home now." I dialed Ris's number first, instantly becoming livid when my call went straight to voice mail. *Childish, absolutely fucking childish.* Yes, I'd blacklisted her number when I left the house with the kids but it was only because I already knew she would call me every five fucking minutes and I didn't want my phone going off all damn day. All it did was send her calls straight to voice mail and any texts she'd send would go to a waiting box. I checked my phone and was surprised when I saw zero voice mails and had zero waiting texts. This was just fucking great; now she wanted to be on some tit-for-tat petty shit by turning off her damn phone.

I dialed Key's number. It rang repeatedly before his voice mail came on. I hung up. It just didn't feel right to leave him a message about my wife missing, not after we'd spent such a nice day together. We'd taken the kids to the park and a duck feeding pond; afterward I sat with the kids and watched movies in his living room while Key was busy in the kitchen making us lunch. That's what a family was supposed to feel like. Not this constant push-pull, give and keep on giving situation I was in, that I had the nerve to be calling a damn marriage.

CHAPTER 18

IF YOU PEE IN RUNNIN' WATER, IT DON'T MAKE NO SPLASH

My phone was completely dead by the time we got to the damn beach. It was a little ways away from the touristy area and quiet, which was good 'cause my ass needed some time to pull it together. I was glad the sun was starting to go down. The humidity was making me sweat up a storm. My borrowed clothes were sticking to my back and my hair was irritating my shoulders. I waited for Lania to pile all her shit back into her purse and we walked toward the ocean, looking for a good spot to sit down. My high was wearing off, the after-effects making me feel a little depressed.

"Want to try something new?"

I wanted to do anything that would make the sad hole in my heart go away. We sat down facing the water and Lania pulled a small white packet from her purse.

"Put a little of this under your tongue, it's better than sex—I promise."

"Shit. I doubt that, but we'll see." I cringed; it was bitter in my mouth like a crushed-up aspirin. "Ugh, you ain't got a Pepsi up in that bitch, do you?"

Lania laughed, dabbing a little of the shit underneath her own tongue. She waved at the ocean. "Water, water all around and not a drop to drink."

We both chuckled and stared out at the sea, waiting for our shit to kick in.

"Lania, you think Key been fuckin' dudes the whole time y'all been together?" I couldn't help it. Maybe the shit was working, making me ask questions I shouldn't be asking but I did. A few minutes passed before she answered me, her words floating to my ears like a song drifting in from the ocean.

"Keyshawn is not gay."

"Um I don't know if you just saw what I saw, but that looked pretty damn gay to me." This bitch was in de-fuckin'-nial.

"Some families have secrets buried so deep that it's the only thing holding the roots in the ground. You pull up those secrets, you loosen the soil, weakening the tree." *Shiiiiiit.* I glanced at Lania's ass out the corner of my eye. *If that wasn't the highest, most poetic shit I ever heard and ain't hardly understand.* I sat there, silently rolling her words through my brain.

"If I tell you something you have to swear you'll never repeat it."

Hell I forgot her ass was sitting beside me for a second. I mean, it's not like I didn't just watch her ass murder a muthafucka' or nothin'—but I guess maybe she wasn't counting that as a real secret, I don't know.
"I promise. I'll even tell you one that you can't say shit about to no-fuckin'-body either."

She nodded, satisfied with our deal. "I owe a huge debt to Angelo Testa. It's the kind of debt that you re-pay for life, until either you die or Angelo dies. You see, I knew him long, long before he became the powerful man he is now."

I waited.

Lania took a shallow breath, her voice shaky as she continued, tears slowly welling up in her golden eyes. "Me and Angelo are bound by the blood of relation. We're brothers."

What the fucccccccccck! The TV audience in my head jumped back to life, screaming in unison as my eyes bulged out my damn head.

"You're . . . I mean . . . you were a man?"

"I'm completely post-op, did hormone injections, pills, all of it. My other brother, Keyshawn, met me long after it was all said and done and I myself never had the heart to tell him different."

The audience's heads tilted to the side in confusion. *Huh? Did he—she—just say . . . No. No.*

"Wait, Lania, you said Keyshawn is your . . . *other brother?*" Boy, these pills was definitely some goooood shit. 'Cause I could have sworn they was putting words in my ears that this bitch's mouth wasn't even saying.

"Right. Keyshawn is my stepbrother by marriage. We were dating and in love way before me and Angelo's mother met Keyshawn's father. We tried to stop seeing each other but it never lasted long, so instead we agreed to just keep a *very, very* open relationship, never revealing our relationship. Key was doing well and shit was going good until he was traded to Miami. Curtis had his eyes on Key the second he stepped out of that locker room. When Key turned him down not too long ago, Curtis started digging for dirt. He was a fool. He paid one of Angelo's goons to dig for him, so we've been feeding Curtis phony information and coming up with dead ends."

I sat there, staring at Lania, captivated. Their story was way more fucked up than the shit Chelle and I had done. No wonder we all got along so well.

"So, what happened back there with Curtis? Wasn't just you on some angry bitch, don't-touch-my-man type shit?"

"Fuck no. Last time I saw Angelo, he told me about a rumor in the owners' box. Something about Curtis wanting to trade Keyshawn to the highest bidder, like fucking livestock."

"That's nothin' new. Players get traded all the time, Lania, it's part of the game."

"True, but Angelo said the rumor also involved Curtis wanting Key injured after the trade so he'd never play again. I told Key about it and apparently he must've cut a deal with Curtis to stay in Miami *and* make more money. No person ever thinks they have a price until someone is willing to pay it. What Key didn't know was that Curtis was going to fuck him and trade him anyway. So, I deaded that shit . . . literally."

It was like hearing the ending of a long, dramatic bedtime story. The sun had almost completely set and every part of Lania's story made sense except for one little-ass piece. "Why would Keyshawn give up da ass just to keep playin' ball? That don't make sense, not when the nigga has the fuckin' Mafia on his side." I had a bitch thinking with that question.

"Only one way to find out."

Oooh, this is gettin' gooood. She whipped out that little phone of hers and dialed Key's number, hitting the speaker button so I could hear everything.

"You got some nerve callin' me right now." Keyshawn's voice came out of the speaker in a loud growl.

Even though it was just over the phone, instinctively, my ass leaned back.

Lania didn't look fazed. "Oh please, boy. I did you a favor and you know it." She started to sing into the phone while making some sorta kissy face. "There isn't even a mess for you to clean up now is there?"

"You already know ya Mafia brother done came over here wit' his fuckin' flunkies and mopped up. What I tell you 'bout callin' dat mu'fucka e'retime some shit go down? I'm tired of havin' blood on my hands, Yylannia."

"*I* kept your hands clean. Now shut up. I have a question," she snapped at him. In the blink of an eye her tone went from soft and playful to razor sharp. "Why did I catch you in the predicament you were in, given we could have resolved this in any number of ways with the snap of a finger and, eh-hmmm, saved your ass, sweetheart?"

We both waited for Key to answer, the phone hanging silently between us like a question mark.

"Because I fuckin' wanted to, Yylannia. You an' your damn brother got a problem with that shit? Huh? I *wanted* to!"

Triple whammy, were the words my mental studio audience shouted at the scene unfolding before me. I looked down and traced a heart in the sand with my finger; I knew exactly how Key must have felt, to have those kinds of feelings and be scared to act on 'em 'cause you afraid of what people might say or think. His family's approval obviously meant a lot to him. I scratched a squiggly break through the heart. That looked a lot better.

"But you told me you turned him down repeatedly and . . . and what about me, Keyshawn? I thought we had an agreement. You seemed happy."

"What about you, Yylannia? There ain't no we, jus' like there could never be anything wit' me an' Curtis. What would the star of the muthafuckin' team look like fuckin' the owner? If that shit got out it would discredit me, ruin my fuckin' career. Jus' like if anyone found out we actually kinfolk. *And, what the fuck was Ris doin' up in here with you?* Angelo know she was wit' you?"

"Of course not, and it doesn't matter, Key."

"So what you think he gon' say when he find out or . . . Oh, lemme guess, y'all cool now, you gon' save her ass too? You trust her like that?"

Lania glanced up at me nervously. I could see her doubting me all of a sudden as Keyshawn continued.

"That shit you pulled was sloppy and reckless, Lania. And, for future reference, I ain't askin' you or anyone else's *permission to use my own gotdamn dick.*" The phone went silent, his growl echoing across the beach out and into the waves.

Someone in the studio audience in my head held up their hand. *Sooooo, you mean to tell me, if Lania, who is a "she" now, woulda just kept her ass as Lance, a "he", then, um, he coulda been on some happily-ever-after shit with Keyshawn fo'reals, 'cause the nigga like dick any damn way?* The rest of the studio audience whistled and cheered and I shook my head. This shit was just too damn much for me. Here I was, all along gettin' jealous over Keyshawn spending time with Michelle and the kids. Thinking that nigga wanted to be *with* Michelle when, in all actuality, that nigga wanted to *be* Michelle.

"You know Keyshawn does have a point, don't you?" Lania was looking down at the sand.

I almost didn't hear her over the conversation I was havin' in my damn head. "Huh? What you say, *Lany?*" Laughin', I nudged her with my shoulder, and the movement made the entire ocean sway with me. "Ooooh, there goes that shit *finalllly* kickin' in. I was startin' to think it was a dud or sumthin'." I looked over at Lania, my mouth opening to ask her if she was okay, and I had to blink to clear the stars from my eyes, my ears suddenly ringing.

"Bitch, you hit me!" I already knew what was goin' on. One of us wasn't gonna leave that beach. Lania done sat there and spilled her fuckin' guts and now after listenin' to Key's ass she was second-guessing shit and trying to clean up after herself. Detroit raised my ass; I knew to throw punches that would break a bitch's nose before I could read or ride a bike.

Lania tried to hit me again and I grabbed her fist, twisting it until she screamed in pain. She grabbed my hair with her free hand and twisted it, tightening it around her fist and pulling my head back until it was in the sand. It felt as though each strand was being torn from my scalp; the pain made me lose my leverage on her hand and I let go. *Fuck, I really wanted to break that shit, too.* Lania climbed on top of me, straddling me, grinning. Her hands wrapped around my throat, and I clawed at the ground, reaching around for something, anything to hit her with and coming up with handfuls of sand.

The bitch laughed, taunting me. "Larissa, what's the matter? You're so pale. You look like you've seen a ghost."

Now I didn't know if black people could actually ever go pale and shit, but I could feel all the blood draining from my face. I stared over Lania's shoulder, tears welling up in the corners of my eyes and sliding down my face, splashing into the sand. I didn't know what the fuck was in that shit Lania gave me. I had to have been higher than the cost of living in California, giraffe pussy, *and* the cost of gas to drive me to the San Diego Zoo to look at the damn giraffe just so I could say, "Damn that pussy high." Because for all intents and purposes, for all my ass knew, I was staring directly at the Ghost of Christmas Past. And it was staring down at me, directly over Lania's shoulder, with a pistol pointed dead center at my muthafuckin' nose. For the first time, the studio audience was completely silent.

CHAPTER 19

DISAPPEARING ACTS

It was going on 2:00 A.M. and no one had bothered returning any of my phone calls. I was debating actually going over to Key's place just to see if maybe they were all over there drunk or high, or worse, having another one of their all-out fuck parties minus me, but I kept talking myself out of it. I refused to embarrass myself in front of him again. Aside from my time in the hospital I couldn't think of one night that Ris and I had spent apart since leaving Virginia. Call it paranoia or intuition, I didn't care; I just had a nagging feeling like something was seriously wrong and it wouldn't go away.

Jim had sent a few of his guys to check the club that we'd been to and a few bars in the area, but since she'd intentionally ditched his team he wasn't too enthused about putting too many man hours into a search at this point. I'd called Keyshawn a few more times and Larissa's phone was still going directly to voice mail. I paced the house top to bottom and nearly jumped outta my skin when my phone rang.

"Keyshawn! Oh my God, Larissa—"

"So, I'm guessing I owe you some kinda explanation huh?" He cut me off before I could finish. He sounded tired, stressed.

"An explanation? About what?" *What the hell is this nigga talkin' about?*

"Wait, huh? I dozed off, I just woke up. What . . . what were you saying about Larissa?"

"Oh, God, Key, I think something's wrong. She left with Lania and a bunch of girls earlier today and I haven't seen or heard from her since."

"Woooow. I mean. You know how they are. So you haven't gotten a text, voice mail, no nothing?" He sounded strange, like he was amused or relieved, I couldn't tell. Maybe he was just happy that I was pissed with Ris because it would give him a chance to get in better with me.

"She's never done anything like this before. *Ever.* I don't know what to do right now. I'm losing my mind over here."

"You know it's fuckin' funny 'cause I haven't heard from Lania's ass all day either; her phone's been off too. You don't think the two of them . . . Nah." He cut himself off.

"Tell me, Keyshawn. The two of them what? What do you know?"

"Shit, don't quote me on this, but Lania had mentioned before that Keisha, the chick from the club—"

"Oh you mean the chick who was with ol' girl. Chanel, the one who was givin' you a hand job under the table?" I couldn't let that one slide. For him to be so interested in havin' me play the lead he sure did seem to have a lot of side tricks lined up waitin' to step in an' take the spotlight. The nigga definitely had ho tendencies and that was definitely a red flag in my book.

"Ah, that was when you was givin' me a hard time remember? I didn't even know I had a real chance wi'chu at that point. But nah, whenever Lania be on that phone off bullshit she's usually up to no good, and after the day I had wi'chu and the kids I gave her ass permanent walkin' papers. No more open relationship. I don't want that lifestyle anymore. I wanna build on somethin', I want a family—somethin' solid."

I was speechless. It honestly wasn't what I expected to hear, but everything I needed. "You know, comin' from a man, words ain't shit to me, Keyshawn. Far as I know you jus' another nigga promisin' me heaven, and for all I know you gonna take me through hell to get there. I got enough hell right now. I can't do this shit anymore."

"You won't have to. How 'bout I come keep you company—we can wait on Ris to call or not call, come home or whatever together. Either way you won't be doin' it by yourself. I make some mean hot cocoa, gurrrrl."

I laughed, I couldn't help it. Something about him just made me happy and the fact that he could do it even at a time like this, when I was actually worried sick outta my mind, made it that much more meaningful.

"Okay, you can keep me company, and I like marshmallows in my cocoa."

CHAPTER 20

UNFORGETTABLE
AIN'T IRREPLACEABLE

Almost a month had passed since Ris walked out of my life leaving the kids, her clothes, and everything we had together. There was always a shadow of doubt in the back of my mind that still carried the slightest fear that maybe something had really happened to her. It would nag me whenever my mind had a chance to wander, like when I was cooking, or taking a shower, or in those last few moments just before I'd fall asleep.

Lania had turned up within the next few days according to Keyshawn. She'd called him hung over and still high, claiming that Ris was of course laid up with that Keisha girl he'd mentioned. I was hurt, but Key turned out to be my knight in shining armor, gluing the pieces of my family back together little by little, even while dealing with the murder of Curtis, who I later found out was like his mentor, according to his team-mates and all the news reports I'd read. They'd found parts of Curtis's body when some trappers caught a gator with a human arm in its mouth about a week after Ris disappeared. They never caught the killer or found the rest of his body; hell the only way they even knew it was Curtis was by his damn fingerprints. I could tell it still really bothered Keyshawn sometimes.

I'd decided to surprise him and make veal parmesan with bacon-wrapped asparagus for dinner. Closing my eyes I let myself enjoy something that I didn't get too often: a quiet house. The kids were at the park with Key, taking advantage of having him around since it was the off-season. I was in the middle of crushing garlic when that all-too-familiar alarm chimed on my iPhone. I hadn't heard from Jim in a while. Keyshawn insisted that I didn't need him since he had his own "special security" that he refused to tell me about. But until I knew Rah was back behind bars I kept Jim on standby.

"Hi, Jim, long time no hear."

"Ye know they say no news is good news. Well I've got some info that'll pro'ly have ya doin' a jig or what-not."

"I'm ready." I took a deep breath, not sure if it would be about Larissa or Rasheed, but anxious either way.

"Not gonna sugarcoat this—they found Rasheed's body yesterday a few miles south of Emporia back in Virginia. Was burned up pretty bad; had to use dental records to identify it. He was inside one of those CMA CGM shipping containers. There was another corpse in there with 'im, one of 'em a female, but we're still waiting on more information. No ID on the Jane Doe as of yet. But I know you'll sleep better now knowing he ain't after ye."

I was dumbfounded. There were tears in my eyes from both sadness and joy.

"He wasn't alive . . . when they burned him, was he, Jim?" No one deserved that kind of death. Not even Rah.

"Not sure yet, sweetheart. We'll know more in a couple of days. I'll give you a ring back. 'Til then you be safe and enjoy yourself now."

I didn't know what to do with myself. I left the food and everything in the kitchen and walked out the front door; the humidity made sweat bead on my forehead almost instantly. I inhaled, smelling the rain that was coming and the rose bushes on the side of the house that'd just started to bloom. The sky was dark from the approach of one of our usual evening thunderstorms and for the first time in months I was able to just enjoy standing outside, not worrying about who, or if someone, was watching me or waiting.

"Woman, you got this house smellin' good." Key walked in right on time with Lataya in his arms and Trey following not too far behind him.

I'd already set the table and was just keeping everything warm until they got back. Fresh basil, garlic bread, bacon; yes, it did smell good and my stomach growled in agreement.

"Everybody wash their hands, it's time to eat."

He came over and gave me a soft kiss, handing me a small pink and white envelope.

"What's this baby?" I looked at it, amused; he never failed to amaze me.

"Oh I don't know, let's open it later." Winking playfully he marched off to the hall bathroom to help the kids wash their hands.

The storm started to roll in just as we finished up dinner. The thunder and lightning were scaring the kids and Keyshawn wasn't helping, jumping and yelling, "Boo," in between every damn thunderclap. This was probably one of the worst ones we'd had all summer; it was going on nine and it still hadn't let up.

"Mommy, can we sleep wif you?" I looked at Key and sighed. *Damn and double damn because this is definitely some of that good old-fashioned handling business weather.*

"Yes, baby. Let's go get our PJs on." Glancing at Key, I led Trey to his bathroom.

He gave me a wink and my ass got excited. That shit meant, *oh we are gonna wait 'til they fall asleep and then the business is gonna get handled.* It didn't take long before all four of us were cuddled up in the bed and the three of them, with their bellies full, were of course unconscious before ten-thirty. Lataya was lying on Keyshawn's chest and Trey was all up in my back when I remembered the envelope he'd given me. I'd left it on the counter downstairs and now my curiosity was getting the better of me.

The storm was still on ten and I couldn't believe the thunder didn't wake the kids up. I'd stopped to look out the window and my mind couldn't help drifting to Larissa. We used to love to watch lightning storms together. "Nature's fireworks" was what she always called them. An exceptionally bright pinkish silver fork split down from the sky and I wondered if she was watching it now.

My phone dinged from its docking station on the kitchen counter. Slipping the small envelope into the top pocket of my pajama top, I checked my phone. It showed I had one missed call. Secretly, I hoped it was Ris. Every time I dialed her number it went to voice mail. Even though she was on my account, I never turned her line off, even though I pretty much assumed she'd probably gotten a new phone by now. I didn't know why I didn't just disconnect it. The missed call was Jim and I pressed the play button to listen to the voice mail he'd left me.

"Hey, Michelle. Funny thing. Was on the phone with the coroner's office in Virginia going over a few details.

The body was set on fire after death. There was no burn or scar tissue on the inside of his lungs."

Well that was good; the last thing I wanted to think about was Rasheed suffering a painful, horrible death. He had a ton of enemies and I could only imagine who would do something like that once they got a hold of him.

Jim's voice mail went on: "Only problem is, tissue samples show massive decomposition. That man been dead for about three, maybe four months. Somebody got a hold of him and took him out *soon* as he got busted out of that prison, Michelle. So my question to you is—"

My iPhone slid from my hand, the glass shattering on the tile of the kitchen floor just as lightning split the sky open and thunder crashed so loud it sounded like a tree trunk being split in half like a twig. I didn't need to hear the rest of Jim's question because the answer was standing in my kitchen, soaking wet, staring me in the face. Rasheed was already dead but this could be the night I was going to die too.

CHAPTER 21

IF I SHOULD DIE BEFORE I WAKE . . .
(Two years earlier, December 25 . . .)

"Okay, sweetheart, you gotta trust me on this shit." Kita was a third-year medical school student who'd been workin' in the women's ward at the prison to finish up her residency or whatever the fuck they called it. She was one of the few people who actually took really good care of me during my pregnancy. She felt the worst 'bout what happened to initially even get my ass locked up, and e'reday when she could see me by myself all we'd talked 'bout was findin' a way to legally get my case appealed. When dat fell through an' every appeal I turned in got turned down, she started tryin' to find ways for me to get out illegally. Kita could lose her financial aid and all her school shit by doin' this, so even though my ass was scared as hell I wasn't gonna let her down.

"This is some experimental shit we been workin' on in lab back at Old Dominion. We've tried it a few times on animals, small pigs, and I'm gonna write my thesis on it and maybe earn myself an article in the *Medical Journal*. It's gonna slow down your heart jus' long enough for you to flat line. It disrupts the electrical transmitters that the EKG machine picks up on. But never mind; that shit's technical. Anyway, in three hours you'll go right back to normal. You still gon' be breathin'; it'll jus' be *extremely* shallow. So shallow nobody will even be able to notice."

We were sittin' in the post-delivery intensive care ward, if that's what you wanna call it. It was really just an area of the prison that they'd sectioned off with a few raggedy-ass hospital beds that had curtains in between 'em, but since there weren't a whole lot of pregnant women up in there it was pretty much all mine. A few days ago I'd been stabbed in my cell by my cellmate— the shit sent me into labor a couple weeks prematurely, but me and my baby were both some fighters and we made it out okay.

Kita was still goin' in, explainin' the plan to get me out. A plan she'd come up with one day outta the blue after my last appeal was finally turned down an' a few of the other inmates started gettin' hostile toward me.

Some shit went down where some of Rah's product was supposed to be killin' people out on the street. They was up in here takin' they anger out on me 'cause I was picked up wit' a loaded car full of his shit, even though my ass ain't even know it was there. But shit like that doesn't matter on the streets. When somebody lose a junkie cousin, brother, or auntie to some bad dope, first thing they wanna do is take out anyone they think coulda gave it to 'em. My question was always why couldn't they ass be as gung-ho 'bout takin' the damn needle or pipe *from* the person as they was 'bout takin' someone's life *over* that person?

"It'll be jus' like havin' one of those dreams where you can't move an' shit but you'll be able to hear an' feel everything."

Damn, she is still goin'. I needed to pay attention. I nodded, intent on keepin' my ass focused this time. The baby ripped me wide da fuck open wit' her water-head self when she came out. *She ain't get that big ol' thang from me. I'm blamin' all that dome piece on her damn daddy.* I was pretty sure my meds must've been wearin' off 'cause the stitches and the knife wound in my side was all startin' to throb again. Thinkin' about my baby made my eyes burn and I could feel the tears comin'. I started blinkin' quickly, tryin' not to cry, and counted the dirty yellow an' white checkerboard tiles along the ward floor. Some were cracked and peelin' up—others were broken in half, just like my family right now. We were separated and torn all apart. *I'd do anything to hold my li'l girl and my man again. Fuckin' worthless-ass prison bitches threw her in my arms and snatched her away before my blood was wiped off'a her or her umbilical cord was even cut.*

"I'ma need you to be dat bitch, Honey. 'Cause they gonna tag you, bag you, and put yo' ass in the morgue, but you jus' keep thinkin' 'bout yo' li'l girl, okay?"

"I . . . I'm gonna be in there wit' dead bodies?" Jus' thinkin' 'bout not bein' able to move, freezin' inside a dead person storage locker, zipped up inside a body bag gave me chills. I was pro'ly gonna have nightmares 'bout this shit for the rest of my life.

"You'll be fine, Honey. My homeboy is wit' the coroner's office—he know what's up. Javis gonna get to you within the first half-hour of me declaring you dead 'cause you'll need to be put on oxygen ASAP. If we can help it you ain't neva' gonna make it to the freezer. You jus' gonna be in the morgue part—that's where they sit the bodies. Then it's a new ID, new name. New life."

"All right, you know I'ma do what it take to get back to Paris an' Rah. I ain' gonna do shit to get either of y'all caught for helpin' me. I'll even cut the skin off the tips of my fingers, like I seen some of the lifers up in here done did, if I have to so they can neva' link the 'new me' back to the me you talkin' to right now."

"Girl, you jus' find your baby, get to your man, an' live the life you was meant to live."

I closed my eyes, 'cause the pain from everything, from my wounds to my heart, was now too much to ignore, and the thought about the letter Kita had me write to Rasheed a few minutes earlier was just now startin' to sink in. In order for everything to work, everyone, including my love, had to believe I was dead. He could take care of Paris until I healed up and then we could all finally be together as a family. He was gonna be mad as hell at me for scaring him like this—I could already hear him cussin' me out now—but in the end it would all be worth it.

"All right, li'l momma, give me your arm."

Kita dipped a cotton ball in alcohol and I jumped when the cold cotton touched my bare skin. Visions flashed before me of the man I loved smilin' as he looked down for the first time at the li'l girl we'd made. I focused on what I wanted. This prison shit was the bad dream and when I woke up I'd be back waking up back in my normal life.

"You're gonna feel a little pinch. Now start counting backward from one hundred, and when you wake up . . ."

I closed my eyes, holding the image of the baby girl I'd just named and let go of, remembering the smile of the man I'd loved and held on to.

"One hundred, ninety-nine, ninety-eight . . ."

CHAPTER 22

THIS WOMAN'S WORK

I'd sat back an' watched these bitches livin' da life I shoulda been livin', raisin' da family I shoulda been raisin' for too damn long. Patience was not somethin' I was good at but I was learnin' it on a daily basis. Growin' up the old folk used to always say, "when you take things for granted, the things you are granted get taken"; well I was 'bout to do a whole damn lot of takin'. They owed me money, they owed me love, time, and sweat, tears, pain, and they owed me my damn daughter. They took Paris from me an' I'd do anything, an' I mean damn near anything, to get my baby back.

The good thing 'bout bein' dead—or I should say bein' thought of as dead—is you get to learn how people honestly feel. You get to see they actions an' compare all that shit to the words that they'd said to you to keep you faithful or loyal or, in my case, to keep you servin' a sentence for some shit you ain't even deserve to be servin' a sentence for. The whole time I was locked up all I could think 'bout was Rasheed. There was a few times when I called him an' he ain't take my call but I tried to be understanding 'cause he was goin' through so much back then. When I'd finally found a way to get out I almost lost my mind, 'cause the first thing I had to learn when I went lookin' for his ass was that my man's bitch-ass baby momma had done turned 'round an' gotten him locked up! It took e'rething in me to not go after her right then an' there.

Michelle an' Larissa. Michelle an' got-damn Larissa. Larissa, my damn cousin. We s'posed to be blood an' I gotta find out dat she the main reason why I know what the inside of prison walls is like, while she livin' in a fuckin' fairytale castle, pushin' Benzes an' shit. Hell da fuck no. First thing first was to get my money up an' that wasn't hard 'cause Rah had shit stashed in places jus' for shit like this. It was a weird feelin' bein' back in Norfolk without him.

January always reminded me of him. From the crunch and color of the leaves on the ground to the way the wind would blow an' it be so cold it damn near freeze ya skin even through your coat an' jeans. He called it get money weather, 'cause the air smelled crisp like brand new bills. And while lazy niggas was cuffed wit' they boos eatin' and gettin' fat, real niggas was hustlin'—out gettin' what them lazy niggas was passin' up. This weather was made for makin' stupid easy money. I smiled to myself and wished some of that stupid easy money would come to me now.

I went to the house where he stayed wit' his baby momma. It was still empty, thank God. I felt like a ghost; hell I was a ghost—creepin' through the dead grass in the middle of the night an' shit. My breath was comin' out in white clouds and my fingers burnin' in my gloves. His neighborhood always smelled like hickory 'cause all dem niggas out there got fireplaces an' they burn 'em hard in the winter. E'retime I smelled that smell it reminded me of him.

Police tape was still on all the doors an' windows, an' the Feds took e'rething up out the house down to the damn curtains. But I jus' carried my ass round the side like I remember Rah tellin' me.

"Any shit ever go down, a nigga grabbin' the burner from up unda the mattress, and if I can't get to a safe for some go paper, I gotta jus'-in-case stack up unda the li'l cement rain gutta on the side of the crib. Rainy day shit fo' sho'. Honey, a nigga stay ready so he ain't eva' and I mean so he ain't eva' gotta get ready."

Smiling, I crouched down as I got closer to the cement rain gutter on the ground. A few beetles ran from up underneath it when I slid it out the way an' it took me a minute to dig 'cause I forgot to bring somethin' to use an' the ground was half damn frozen. After a good thirty minutes I hit a li'l tin box an' uncovered it enough to get the lid off. He had at least seventy Gs in there and I stuffed it inside of the li'l blue duffel bag I had with me. It ain't have much in it, but it held everything I owned. This was more than enough for what I needed to start; the rest would find its way to me. I just needed to find my way out of Virginia until I could come up with a solid plan; it was too risky stayin' here.

They was both so damn stupid; like changin' names an' movin' all the way down the East Coast and whatnot would keep somebody from findin' 'em. I was gonna pay one of Rah's old homeboys to find 'em but I didn't wanna involve anyone else. So I used a pay phone outside the 7-Eleven not too far from Brambleton Street. Called the Norfolk district court one day pretendin' I was Michelle askin' if they could verify the forwardin' address for Paris's birth certificate. Some Latasha chick, or whoeva' she was, was all like, "Oh we mailed that already." So I said, "Well, ma'am, I ain't get it. Can you please verify where you sent it?" And just like that I knew exactly how to find they asses.

Soon as I knew how to find them, my next move was finding a way to get to Rasheed. I had to be able to pay the guards and COs and still have somewhere to lay my own head at night. I couldn't hang around Virginia to earn money for fear of someone recognizing me. I walked my ass to the Greyhound bus station and bought myself a ticket to Florida.

CHAPTER 23

KINGS AND QUEENS

That had to have been the longest fuckin' bus ride of my life. I was scared to sleep most of the way only 'cause I had so much cash on me an' I ain' want nobody to try to snatch my shit. I spent most the of trip tryin' to figure out how to get Rah out of prison an' the other half tryin' to figure out what to do with Michelle and Larissa in order to get my daughter back. I was stuck sittin' beside Baby Huey the first half of the ride. This fat-ass white corn fed–lookin' mu'fucka. He smelled like mustard and armpit sweat and kept fallin' asleep, snorin' loud as fuck wit' his head back; sounded like he was gonna jus' die. Stuck between his ass and the window was hell, but he got off in North Carolina and it was jus' me after that.

Miami compared to Virginia was a culture shock. It was already damn near sixty-five degrees outside and all over the place everyone looked tan, beautiful, happy. The first thing I did was find a cab to get my ass to the Ritz-Carlton hotel. When I was locked up, we'd see commercials for them hotels and I remembered thinkin' if I ever got up out of there and could do it I'd stay my ass in one of those—well that and I couldn't think of any other fancy places so that was that.

A short, little man with a hat and suit held the door with his white gloves as I walked into the lobby and I was in awe. There was floor-to-ceiling mahogany walls covered in mirrored balls that lit up. Cream-colored leather armchairs were all over the place and everything up in there looked like it cost a damn arm and a leg. There were live exotic flowers and this waterfall and stream with real fish swimmin' in it. The place was like a dream come true and I was only in the damn lobby. I wished Rasheed could've been there with me.

"Welcome to the Ritz-Carlton Hotel, South Beach Miami. Um, may I be of service?"

There was a snooty-lookin' older black woman behind the counter lookin' down her nose at me. "Umm. I'd like your biggest suite please."

"Ma'am, that would be the Ritz-Carlton Suite, it's approximately four thousand dollars per night."

I didn't see this bitch's fingers movin'. "Okay." I just stared at her blankly, and her dumb stuck-up ass just kept lookin' at me. Reachin' into my duffle bag I peeled off twenty Gs and laid the cash on the counter with the fake ID I had made before I left Virginia. I didn't think I'd seen strippers snatch up paper fast as that bitch scraped that shit up off the counter. I laughed—money always talks. But, shit, that was already twenty that I'd just dropped and it was only for a few days. I was gonna need to hustle that shit back, and fast.

"Here is your key. Brighton, will you show Ms. Lacroix to her room?"

It was weird as fuck hearing someone call me by that name. Kita, the girl who helped get me the ID, said it a few times out loud so I'd know how to pronounce it and I'd guess I'd forgotten since then. The desk clerk snapped her fingers and some redheaded white guy appeared beside me in the same uniform as the guy who held the door. He tried to take my bag but I refused, jerking it closer to my side. Fuck that—all my

money was up in there and I had a death grip on it.
Seein' that, he shrugged and led me to the elevator up
to the fifteenth floor where he unlocked my door and
showed me into my suite. I wasn't gonna tip his ass
at first because I ain't have change for a hundred, but
then I remembered when mu'fuckas used to say that
shit to me when I was dancin' and I'd be thinkin', *you
knew you was comin' up in here so why you ain' get
change first?* Plus Rah used to always say to take care
good care of workin' men and women— waitresses,
bus boys, bartenders and shit—'cause you never knew
when you'd need 'em.

"Thank you so very much, Ms. Lacroix." His wrist
went up in the air, and he had this cute little singy
voice. *Aww, he's fam,* I thought, immediately feelin'
homesick. I used to love goin' to the drag shows up
in Nutty Buddy's an' watchin' the queens go in on
some songs. They'd be on stage in heels, makeup, an'
dresses, *killin'it.*

"Now look, this is for our exclusive VIP Ritz guests.
I usually don't give it out because they worry me to
death. Press this little button and talk into the light-up
part and tell me what you need and Brighton will be
your personal genie." He handed me the little silver
radio and sashayed out of the room.

Lookin' around I'd neva' seen anything like this
shit before. To go from the life I lived, basically sellin'
myself on stage dancin' and sweatin' my ass off for a
bunch of strangers, to bein' locked up an' sittin' in a
cell and still having not a damn thing to show for it, to
where I was now. Lookin' out a window at white sand
an' clear blue ocean wit' more money in my hand than
I'd ever seen or made in my entire life was a sign that I
was on the right path. This shit was fuckin' bananas. I
laughed like I was twelve again and jumped up on the

infinity-somethin' cloud bed, sending all the pillows and the blue and gold Egyptian cotton 2,000-thread-count sheets flyin' everywhere. The entire room was decorated in blues and golds and I felt like Cleopatra sittin' in my empire beside the beach.

Tired, I fell out on my back and closed my eyes. Inhaling deep, I took in the smells of the ocean from the large balcony doors, citrus and coconut, and . . . *ugh,* my funky ass.

After my shower I decided to explore. I took $4,000 wit' me along wit' the *Star-Trek*-lookin'-ass communicator Brighton gave me an' locked the rest of the cash up in the safe. The hotel was like a damn mini resort. I stopped and bought myself a cute li'l black an' tan swimsuit outta the gift shop an' went lookin' for the hot tub so I could relax and think. First thing I needed to do was get my ass some clothes. It was a good thing where I was goin' was away from the main lobby and all the guests. The Jacuzzi was in its own area closed off from the main pool. I was crushed when I got in there an' saw the OUT OF ORDER sign on the door. Looked like I'd have to settle for either sittin' in the steam room or the sauna that was right behind it. I poked my head into the sauna first and cringed. The heat was so dry it damn near made my nose bleed so, of course, I picked the steam room. I sat down an' the machine scared the fuck outta me when it cut on fillin' the room wit' steam. The smell reminded me of Vicks VapoRub, but it was still relaxing. It was makin' so much noise and there was so much steam in the room I couldn't hear or see outside the glass doors. When the steam finally stopped I froze at the sound of the voices outside.

"So we gonna meet wit' 'em at the bah an' then what?"

"And then you's follow my lead. He shows us the dope, we show 'em the cash but we ain' givin' that Guido fuck nothin'. We gonna take his shit an' dead his bitch ass."

"What if he don't let it go that easy or he put up a fight?"

"What da ya mean, what if he don't let it go? We make him let it the fuck go. We take this shit tonight and *we,* you an' me, run this shit. This tan, Botox, and tits city will be ours by morning. Bosses don't get made; bosses make themselves. You mark me on that shit."

I stayed my ass as still as possible in that damn steam room. I felt like I was gonna pass out an' hoped they ain' keep talkin' too much longer, but I'd rather die from the steam than from the hands of whoever those two mu'fuckas was. I waited until it got completely quiet before I felt like it was okay to leave. My head was spinnin' from the heat an' I ain' know if I was even gonna make it back to my room, but damn that shit was crazy. I shook my head. *Who the fuck was them two fools tryin' to set up?* That sounded like some straight up VA-dope-boy bullshit. I tell you what—ain't no sunshine in the damn dope game. The game stay on some shady shit no matta where you think you at or what side you on.

I made it to my room, thankful they had cookies an' shit in the lobby; it gave me just enough energy to stop at a boutique I'd noticed earlier to grab a few outfits so I'd have something to wear for dinner. I changed and went downstairs to one of the hotel restaurants to get a steak or something before my ass passed out and to look an' see what kind of strip clubs they had in the area. Damn, I ain't wanna go back to strippin' but I'd have to start somewhere. I was halfway done with my carne asada fries and jumbo mango margarita when

I recognized the voices I'd heard earlier. They were sitting directly behind me, talkin' business at the bar. Turning slightly in my seat I glanced over my shoulder. I couldn't see their faces. I could only see the clean-cut dark-haired white boy they was talkin' to. My heart went out to him—poor dude, he ain't have no idea what he was in for.

"So you meet us an' you ain' bring shit, mudafucka?"

"Maybe. Right now, you ain't showin' me enough to make a ten dolla' hooka' give you a second glance, *figli di puttana*. I got it, just not here."

I remembered hearin' those words a few times from the Italian chicks up in prison. This dude jus' sat there an' not only insulted 'em but he called these dudes "motherfuckers" to their faces. I listened for a few seconds; he was a cocky li'l somebody, reminded me of my baby. Damn, that could have been Rah—doin' some shit tryin' to make money wit' me at home waitin' on his ass an' these bitch-ass mu'fuckas was tryin' to take him for everything he was worth. Dead his ass and walk away with everything he'd worked for.

I had to do something. I pulled out the little radio and put the earpiece in so I could call Brighton. *Damn why didn't this shit come with fuckin' instructions?* It took me a second to figure it out but I finally got that shit.

"How may I help you, Ms. Lacroix?"

"Brighton, enough wit' that Ms. Lacroix shit. Jus' call me Honey—I need a favor." I held the earpiece in my ear, tryin' to keep my voice as low as possible.
"I'm in the Lapidus Lounge. Come get the guy at the bar. He's wearin' the green an' black striped shirt. The one talkin' to the two guys. Tell him he has a phone call in the main lobby."

"Okay, Ms. Honey. You talking about the cute li'l thang who came in with them grey eyes. I'm on it. I'll be right there."

I laid some money on the table an' went up to the front desk an' waited. When he walked out I grabbed his arm an' pulled him over into one of the side hallways.

"Them guys you talkin' to, they gon' take whatever it is you sellin' an' they gonna kill yo' ass. So if I was you—I'd leave now."

The mu'fucka actually laughed dead in my face. "I'm sorry. Excuse me for bein' so rude, beautiful, and who are you again?"

He was still chucklin', and all I could think was that this fool had to be dumb or straight-up crazy before answerin' him. "I'm nobody. Don't you worry 'bout all that. Did you hear what I jus' said?"

"Yes, gorgeous, I heard you." He looked around before leanin' down close to my ear like he had a secret. "That's actually the plan. They's been fuckin' wit' my operation since day one, ground zero. My boys is outside and when they make they move—we gonna' make ours. Bada boom bada bing,It's finished."

Well damn, I thought, *so much for tryin' to help; men always thinkin' they got they shit together.*

"So once again I'm askin' who's this li'l guardian angel who woulda saved my life, if it'd needed savin'?"

I looked up into the clearest grey eyes that I'd ever seen in my life an' all I could think was, *Damn, his eyes is sexy as fuck.* "Once upon a time, my name was Honey."

And that's how I met King Angelo Testa, the boss of Miami.

CHAPTER 24

BITTER HONEY

It didn't take me long to confide in Angelo. Eventually I broke down and told him every last detail 'bout my situation. In a way he felt as though he owed me a favor because if he was really in some shit an' hadn't known those guys were gonna set him up, I woulda gotten him out of it. When I finally told him everything that I wanted to do as far as gettin' my daughter back, he offered to let me stay wit' his cousin Tink out in Miami until I could get my money up an' get to Rasheed. He even came up wit' a way for me to get Rah outta prison. I worked wit' his sister Lania escortin', and did li'l odds an' ends bullshit here an' there until I was finally ready. It took me almost two years before I had enough money stacked up.

I flew to Virginia and put in a call to a couple of the COs out there just to test the waters and see who would play for money and who wouldn't. Most of 'em was scary as hell so it took a lot of fishing before I found any who were willin' to bite. When a couple of the K-9 trainin' officers were out in a bar one night drinkin', I decided to start buyin' rounds an' askin' questions. Recent freezes in pay raises and overtime cuts had 'em all a little salty and hard up for extra cash. It was nothing to throw 'em a couple thousand just to give me a few details on how the dogs are escorted in an' out, sick not sick, et cetera.

Findin' a CO to help Rah get out was actually easier than I thought it was gonna be, an' I shoulda known somethin' was up wit' that shit from the start. I had done the same thing as before. Hung out in a bar that the female COs went to and asked 'bout his ass. One CO, big ugly-ass heffa, was all like, "Oooh if I could get his fine ass," et cetera. So, end of the night I catch her outside an' offer her $50,000—half up front, the other half after he's out. She accepts and I tell her the plan and where to meet me. I pick a spot all the way out in Emporia, damn near in the country, away from the city, where I have a car hidden and everything. I let her know to leave him there, emphasis on the word *leave*.

I didn't trust no damn body after the shit Larissa an' Michelle pulled so I watched from one of the towers with another guard I'd paid. I saw when that big-ass Andre the Giant–lookin' bitch put Rasheed in that damn dog crate. I was parked nearby when she got outside the prison walls an' she let him out the crate. My heart hit the floor when he laughed, pulled her close, and they kissed. Yeah, I saw it all. Rah grabbed this ugly bitch ass an' was huggin' all up on her an' shit before he got in the passenger side of the car.

They were joy ridin' down the fuckin' road, stoppin' to get coffee an' junk food. I was followin' 'em the whole time. It took everything in me to just be still when they was stoppin' at hotels to fuck. Rah was probably tellin' her he loved her and whatever else she need to hear 'cause he thinkin' all this shit was on her, not knowin' someone else financed his freedom. They finally got to Emporia, to an address I gave her off a red clay-dirt road with a gravel driveway. It was actually an old abandoned house that I'd had decorated just so I could meet my man for the first time in two years. I'd handpicked out li'l shit like sheets and pillowcases. makin' sure there were steaks to cook for breakfast along wit' his steak sauce. I parked an' walked up, 'cause you can't drive on a gravel driveway without makin' noise. The way they was goin' at it the entire time I wasn't surprised when I walked in while they were fuckin'. Her big ass was sweatin' and ridin' him hard as hell. I closed the door behind me and stood there for a few minutes until Rasheed saw me. The look on his face was like he mentally shat a brick. Of course the CO's big ass didn't bother gettin' up.

I stood right there and I asked him, while his dick was still in her and e'rething, "So who you love, Rasheed? The bitch who done died an' paid to get you outta prison or the bitch who can put yo' ass right back?"

He looked at me and back at her. "What the fuck? I . . . They t . . . told me. Oh my God." He was lookin' exactly like he'd seen a damn ghost. Hell, everybody'd been lookin' at me like that; I was gettin' used to that damn look.

"No, nigga it ain't God. It's Honey." I watched the man I thought I loved so much debate between a life in prison—because he knew if he said he loved me that CO was gonna act like her ass had found him and take him right back to that prison so damn fast—and me . . . Well he already knew if he ain't say it was me . . .

"Honey, I thought you was dead. They had a funeral an' everything. It's been damn near two years. What the fuck you think a nigga was gonna do?"

"Okay, baby. Is that yo' answer then?"

He was starin' at me, wide-eyed, brain whirrin', tryin' to spin me one of his famous "save a nigga" stories but too much time behind bars had slowed down that fast-ass mouth of his. Back in da day the nigga woulda told me some shit that woulda had me thinkin' I was wrong for havin' the nerve to even walk in the damn room while he was fuckin' somebody else. I shook my head at him.

His lack of an answer was all the answer I needed.

"I went to prison, Rasheed. I had our daughter. I died, came back, sold my body, some of my soul, gave up things I can never get back. And you can't even look this bitch-ass correctional officer in the face an' say you love me over her ass outta fear that you gon' be locked back up!" I was done wit' both they asses.

"I could have her dead before she could even take you back, Rasheed, but fuck both y'all. You ain't even worth it to me anymore." I didn't know where the tears came from, but they were there. Tiny streams runnin' down my face, blurrin' my vision. It was one thing to dream and see us together but it was another thing to have all this shit shattered by the one mu'fucka who put the hope there to begin with. I'd opened the door to leave and almost screamed at the figure in front of me. I wasn't expectin' him to be standing there and it scared the fuck out of me. When I realized what his being there meant, I almost screamed for him to just leave.

"Angelo, what'chu doin' here?"

"Came to make sure you was good, princess." Head tilted to the side, muscles tensed, him and Rasheed was in a stare down.

"Really, Honey, you come up in here wit' the new nigga, worried 'bout what the fuck I'm doin'?"

"Rasheed, you don't know who you're talkin' to. Jus' shut up." I didn't even look in Rah's direction as I spoke. I was starin' in Angelo's grey eyes. They were cloudy like a storm was comin'. The muscle in Angelo's jaw was clenchin' and I put myself between him an' Rasheed, my hands up on Angelo's chest, trying to calm him down, but it was too late. Angelo's pistol was already drawn; they were both dead behind me before I could turn back around. I could smell gunpowder and the metallic coppery odor from all of the blood.

"I knew you would show that *figlio di una cagna—* son of a bitch—too much mercy, sweetheart." He lifted my chin, staring me in the eyes. "You won't make the mistake again will you?"

All I could do was shake my head no, stunned, dazed, speechless. I couldn't turn around. I didn't want to see Rasheed and that bitch laid out. Didn't want to be stuck with the visions of the brain splatter, blood, none of that shit. Revenge I wanted, yes, but the silent rage and cold mindset that someone needed to make that kind of shit happen was where I just didn't have the stomach.

"Good, baby doll." He wrinkled his nose. "I got the boys outside; let's get them to put the bodies in the container, and get the fuck outta this Podunk countryass town. My woman's been hell bent on revenge an' neglecting her man." He leaned down and kissed me softly, my eyes closing by themselves at the touch of his lips.

CHAPTER 25

CAT AND MOUSE

Now that Rasheed was no longer an option or an idea or a dream, my next step was figuring out what to do with these damn thorns in my side, aka Larissa and Michelle. The flight back to Virginia was quick and painless. I was standing in the doorway of what would be Paris's bedroom. We'd gotten a crib and a bed and I'd picked out a sheep-skin fur rug that sat in the middle of the room. In the corner was her toy box, already full of brand new toys and baby dolls. I had no idea what size she was wearin' now so I was gonna wait and get all of her clothes after we picked her up.

"Tink say you spend more time standin' here starin' off into space than you do lookin' at the ocean."

I didn't even hear him come up behind me. I leaned myself back into his chest and tried to relax for once. "You think she gonna like the Gucci bedspread? It isn't pink but I'd heard you can do yellow for little girls, too." I couldn't make up my mind on the colors to pick out for her room. Since the house was so open to the ocean and the beach, pink and all that girly shit just didn't feel like it went well. I'd decided to go with soft yellows and oranges to complement the views of the ocean.

"*Il mio amore,* our little angel is goin' to adore any- and everything that you give her. I promise. Now stop. You worry too much."

He was right. I was worryin' 'bout all the wrong shit. I needed to start plannin' out exactly how I was gonna get to her and then get the ball rollin' on gettin' Paris back home.

"By the way, good news. Lania says her brother set up that meetin' with this Michelle woman. They'll be meeting him to look at a house and get things goin' next week. The mark is set; you ready this time?"

I thought about it for a split second. Was I ready to see the joy of my life again after two years? Yes. Was I ready to face the two bitches who'd taken her ass from me and deliver justice as Angelo had done with Rah? I wasn't too sure about that shit. I sucked it all up and straightened my shoulders. "I'm ready, baby."

The plan was simple. Lania was there to bait Larissa and Keyshawn's job was to bait Michelle. It was Angelo's idea to approach them on some divide and conquer–type shit instead of just goin in guns blazin' and wrecking shop.

"We gonna cat an' mouse these bitches, and when just when they think shit's at its worst, when they finally sayin', 'Oh my God, I can't do this anymore,' we gonna fall da fuck back. We'll wait until they sittin' there in they comfy li'l worlds, thinkin' they just dodged a bullet—then we gonna smack they asses like we the hand of God Himself."

Since neither one of they asses had any idea that I was still alive, it was gonna to be easy to bait and reel them in once they found out Rah was dead. Angelo kissed the side of my neck. I didn't think I'd ever get used to dealing with an Italian dude. It's not that his breath stank or anything like that. He just always smelled like garlic; the semi-sweet odor was always all over him. It even came out of his pores when he sweat.

Reaching down he cupped my ass in his hands. *I ain't feel like fuckin' this nigga, not right now.* It was like I'd traded the stripper pole for a long, skinny Italian one. Yeah, this one came with perks like money and power. When we went out people respected me simply 'cause they knew I was with King, but what I had for Rasheed was true, genuine love. This shit was just another job in my mind, and I couldn't wait until the day came when I could get promoted or better yet be my own damn boss.

Turning around I looked up into his eyes; they was the most attractive thing about him aside from his money. This fool had definitely fallen in love with me, it was written all over his face. Anything I wanted was mine; all I had to do was think about it and he'd make it happen. He'd do anything to make me happy.

"You wanna go upstairs, baby?" I already knew what his answer was gonna be. I could feel his long pencil dick already gettin' hard up against my stomach. *Why couldn't that shit be thicker? Then it would be perfect. Hell I'd take short an' fat as fuck over long and skinny any damn day.* Sex wit' Angelo was like bein' poked over and over with a long skinny finger. Then this fool wanna be doin' acrobatic shit, liftin' my legs and all kinds of foolishness; sometimes it would feel like he was stabbin' me in my fuckin' kidneys.

"I can't, *bella,* I've gotta go handle some business. But when I get back home best believe papa will be *handling business.*"

I breathed a sigh of relief and thankfully he mistook it for disappointment. At least while he was gone, I could go and get things rolling with Michelle and Larissa—maybe I'd get to see my baby.

***

I decided to take Angelo's silver Monte Carlo as planned. It was the one with the headlights that looked like blue beams of light when they was lit up. That shit was so sexy. It was decked out, too, with silver, grey, and black marble interior and all-black leather. It came with all this extra shit that I ain't have no idea how to use, OnStar navigation and whatever else. Long as that bitch went into drive and got me where I needed to go I was good.

I followed the address that the court had given me and drove the forty-five minutes from Miami to Fort Lauderdale where they lived. I couldn't help feeling awestruck as I parked across the street from a big-ass red brick two-story house with double glass doors on the front. The house was fuckin' huge; it was more long than it was tall, and had windows on one part that went from the ground all the way up. I wasn't completely sure about what I was gonna do until I saw her.

Tears were filling my eyes and it took everything in me not to jump outta the car right then and there. I'd missed so much, her first teeth, first smile, first words and steps. She was so short. I laughed. Hell I wasn't that tall my damn self but I was hoping maybe she'd have gotten a little height from Rasheed. But she was standing beside Trey, who looked like he'd shot up like a damn bean sprout. Her fat little legs were pumping, trying to keep up with him. She tripped and I thought she was gonna cry but she, my big girl, surprised me; she just got back up and started runnin' again.

Larissa came out the front door, saying something to the kids from the porch but I couldn't make it out. I guessed she'd told the kids to come inside, and they weren't moving fast enough. She stormed off the porch, yankin' Paris up by her arm, smackin' her butt, an' then smackin' Trey in the back of the head as he walked past her. Nothing could have prepared me for seein' my child being handled so harshly by another woman an' not bein' able to do nothin' about it. It was time for this shit to start. I pulled a piece of paper out of the glove compartment and grabbed a pen. It jus' so happened to be red, which was perfect, because my ass was out for blood.

CHAPTER 26

RIGHT WHERE WE LEFT OFF. . .

Havin' Lania on the inside was a huge plus. I figured Michelle would go to some extremes once she got scared, but this whole security company shit was a bit hard to get around. They weren't hard to spot, though; you don't miss big-ass white dudes sittin' in cars twenty-four hours a day outside someone's house. One random day I'd decided to swim my ass back around the house just so I could get a look at what we were workin' with from the other side. Angelo took us out on one of his boats, and instead of sailing by the house and looking all suspicious, we dropped the anchor a few miles away and I swam. I'd tied my hair up and put on a wetsuit. It took me damn near an hour to get directly behind they house. Michelle was out there in the pool. I could see a third-level window back there, one that we couldn't see from the front. It looked like someone could climb up to it pretty easily. I was so excited about that window I sputtered and swallowed a mouthful of nasty-ass salt water, when I looked back down at the pool and saw Michelle looking right back at me. It had to be next to impossible for her to see me, but I dove and swam my ass away as many yards underwater as I could. I didn't come up until my lungs felt like they was about to explode.

When Keyshawn told me it was Michelle who'd crashed and almost died in the wreck and not Larissa I was in complete shock. There was no way that flashy piece of shit convertible was Michelle's car; she wasn't into shit like that. It had my cousin's name written all over it. Angelo found Candi, through one of his boys; she was loyal, young, and a straight-up little tomboy grease monkey. I told her a hundred times to make sure there weren't no car seats or no toys or shit like that in the car she fucked up. We ain't count on the babysitter seeing her when she was trying to leave. But Angelo was in good with everyone in Miami, it wouldn't take but so many phone calls and so much hand washin' or passin' money to get her cleared.

The whole car routine was really just to scare they asses. I was hoping Larissa would get banged up and then I could get her while she was in the hospital on some real dramatic-type angel of death shit. Unplug her life support, put somethin' in her IV, I didn't know. According to Angelo, the bitch was doing side jobs with Lania and her girls. I couldn't help smirking at that shit. The thought of Larissa hoin' herself out was a mess, enough to make me damn near piss myself. Now that we knew she was gettin' close to Lania it would be nothing to get her off by herself and handle business.

I stood over her now with the barrel pointed at her head.

"You look a li'l surprised, cuzzo, but it's nice seein' you too. Get your ass up." I didn't know what kinda shit Lania had them trippin' off of. She and all them model bitches stayed high off something. Larissa stood up, looking at me like she couldn't tell if I was a hallucination or a some kind of monster back from the dead.

"You dead, Honey. Either this some kinda voodoo-zombie shit or I'm havin' the craziest fuckin'. . . Lania, can . . . can you see this bitch too?"

I almost laughed at her dumb ass. I don't know why we wasn't filming that shit. Keepin' the gun on my target I turned my head in Lania's direction. "Lania? You good? Can you drive yourself home or I need to get someone to take you?" She was still sittin' in the sand lookin' like her world had ended or her heart was broken, I could never tell wit' her overly dramatic ass. Angelo told me all 'bout the little fucked-up love affair she was havin' with her stepbrother and shit. She was the main reason why he was so fuckin' timid and on the fence when it came to gettin' Michelle where we needed her. Some kind of brother-sister power struggle they all seemed to stay goin' through.

"I'm good. You're going to finish this now are you not?" She weaved where she stood, looking at me expectantly as if she didn't already know my answer.

"I am. This shit ends today."

Lania staggered to her feet and walked back in the direction I'd seen them approach from earlier.

"Honey, please, I'm sorry. We ain't mean to do shit to you. You just got caught up in—"

"Y'all ain't mean to get me locked up? What the fuck you think was gonna happen when you called and reported that car Rah gave me?" I stared at her, half expecting a real logical heartfelt answer, knowing her ass ain't have one.

"Honey, it was Rasheed we wanted to fuck up, ma. Not you. You don't wanna do this shit."

"The fuck you gonna tell me what I do an' don't wanna do? You don't even know *what* I'm gonna do."

"Anything you want you got it, just say the word. If I can't make it happen I'll find someone who can."

I couldn't hide the sneer that spread across my face. *Amazing how people will promise you shit they ain't got and don't even know if they can get when they got a gun pointed at their head.*

"There's nothing you can give me that my new man, Angelo, hasn't."

Even though her ass was high she knew what that name meant comin' out of my mouth. "How the fuck you get connected like that?" She whispered it, more like a thought out loud than a question directed at me.

"I want my daughter and I don't need *you* to get her back. All the times I sat and watched you put yo' hands on my child, like you was disciplining a damn dog. The way you talked to her."

Shock was written on her face. She didn't know I knew about the abuse, the welts, the bruises. The way she talked to the kids when Michelle wasn't around. From what I remembered Larissa couldn't stand kids, never really could. She just played the mommy role around Michelle's ass and that was it. Nothing could have prepared me for the anger that seared through me in a heated flash. The nozzle flared on the silencer, and I watched the shock in her eyes change to fear and then pain as she fell down onto the sand, holdin' her side.

"I ain' mean nothin' by it. How my momma and grandma raised me, even how Grandma did you. Remember? I ain't know no different."

She stared up at me until the pain faded from her eyes, until they were no longer the bright green I always remembered. Blood ran down the sand toward the ocean and I watched the trail for a second, wondering if I was gonna be just as bad with Paris because of how I was raised. I vaguely remembered being ordered to pull switches from rose bushes with the thorns still on 'em. Gettin' whoopin's across my bare legs because I'd fallen asleep in church or back talked. Extension cords, yardsticks, and flip-flops were regular weapons of ass destruction because we was always gettin' into something and doing shit we usually had no damn business doing.

"Good job; you are making me more and more proud each day. Pretty soon you'll be cold and calculated enough to be your own *capo*." Angelo had been watching me from the sidelines as usual, just in case I'd gotten cold feet again. He ain't have to worry about that shit happening, not when my daughter was involved.

"As much as I like it when you talk that talk, I have no idea what that means, baby." He always mixed that Italian shit in when he spoke and sometimes I could pick it up, but I'd never heard him use that word before.

"*Capo* means boss. You lookin' like a beautiful angel of death right now."

Boss. I liked the way that sounded comin' from his lips. I still had one more mu'fucka on my list to show exactly who's boss.

CHAPTER 27

SAVE THE BEST FOR LAST

After takin' care of Larissa's ass we had to chill for a minute so Angelo could cover up the sloppy work Lania did on Curtis. She was gonna get herself fucked up in the game if she ain't stop takin' all that shit an' then runnin' around makin' stupid decisions. Keyshawn was supposed to be keeping his eye on Michelle but something told me by the way he rarely checked in with Angelo, and how Lania seemed to stay upset with him, he was fallin' off. One of us needed to make a move before that nigga's puppy-lovin' ass slipped up and decided to either tell Michelle wassup or get her out the area.

It was one of those random days in August when Angelo hit me, letting me know they'd found the bodies in Emporia. That meant Michelle's little security team would probably be giving her the news that Rah was dead. Which meant it was time for me to make my move, end this shit for good, and get my child. All I could think about was holding and kissing her little chubby face. I walked up to the side of the house, pissed that it just so happened to be raining buckets from the damn sky. I was soaked, but I wasn't gonna let a little rain keep me from doing this shit. Lightning split the sky open as I thought this through one last time.

The back door was unlocked, just as planned. I was glad Keyshawn didn't back out on his word. Angelo was already on the verge of havin' that nigga killed just for GP. I let myself in as quietly as possible, the thunder coverin' up any little noises I might have accidentally made. I'd only been standing there for a few seconds when she came floatin' up into the kitchen, tall and regal. I'd always envied her. She was wearin' a man's red and blue checkered pajama shirt without the bottoms and her hair was tied up in a little scarf.

I looked at this other woman, who had captured the heart of my man and then thrown it away like it wasn't more than an empty soda can. Watching Michelle was like watching Snow White fuck around in the forest with all those damn animals. She floated over and looked at this, then floated over to look at her phone, before fluttering to pick up something else. It was like the bitch moved around in a dream bubble. I'd had enough of watching her flutter around the kitchen and stepped forward out of the shadows and into her line of vision.

"You look so shocked to see me. I was maybe hoping for—happiness."

She just stood there as her phone broke, glass scattering into a million pieces all over the floor. I could see her ass debating: run or fight; scream for Keyshawn or grab a kitchen knife. I shifted the gun from my right hand to my left, reminding her it was in my hand just in case she'd forgotten.

"You don't know how to speak to your house guests— offer 'em a glass of water or a dry towel, Michelle?"

"Legally she's my daughter. I've done everything for her—all the things you never could have done, even loving her like she was my own child. I've been doing it all, Honey."

What she was saying shocked me, and especially the way she said it, nothing like Larissa's dumb-ass begging and bartering. Michelle actually cared about Paris, that much was obvious.

"I'm tired of y'all bitches tryin'a tell me what the fuck I can and couldn't or will and won't do. You don't know *what* I can do now, Michelle."

"Honey, all I'm tryin' to say is that I took care of your daughter the best I knew how. I've raised Lataya right along wit' Trey like she was my own, at no point did I do for one and not do for the other."

"Who the fuck is Lataya? My daughter's name is Paris. Here yo' ass done renamed my child an' everything, what gave you the got-damn right, Michelle? And where were you when Larissa was out there talkin' to her like she wasn't nothin' but a damn dog? Where was you when she was puttin' her hands on my daughter, Michelle?"

She was starin' at me, tryin' to put the meaning to my words. "She'd never . . . Larissa wouldn't do anything like that."

"It's a shame you got cameras all up in here and still don't even know what's going on in your own damn house." I waved the gun, directing her to carry her ass through the door toward the car waiting outside.

"Wait, what about Trey? What's gonna happen to my child with me gone?"

Honestly I didn't feel like she deserved any kind of an answer; my ass didn't get one when they took my child away from me. "Rasheed's momma back in Virginia gonna keep him. Y'all took a lot from a whole lot of people on some straight-up selfish bullshit. His momma been depressed, not eatin', and everybody been worried about her. Having Trey and a little extra money might actually pull her out of the slump she in. Help balance shit back out."

"Can I tell him good-bye?" She had tears all up in her eyes and I almost felt sorry for her. Almost.

"You already know the answer to that. It's no. Now get ya ass outside. You ain' 'bout to get us off schedule."

CHAPTER 28

DON'T BE SO DAMN
SMART ALL THE TIME

I let Honey lead me out of the house, rain soaking through my nightshirt and plastering my hair down to my face and forehead. She forced me into the back of a silver Audi. Looking through the rain-streaked rear window I stared at the house. It would probably be the last time I ever saw it and I tried to remember every detail. Before pulling off she leaned over the seat and roughly handcuffed my hands together in front of me. In a sense I guessed I'd earned this shit. Larissa and I had played God, deciding who deserved to be met with what punishment; we altered peoples' lives and now everything was coming back on our asses full circle.

As the car started to pull forward I couldn't resist questioning Honey. I had no idea how she'd gotten out or how she'd found us. "So I'm guessing it was you who murdered Rasheed?" I knew her ass heard me. She was squinting through the windshield, trying to navigate us to wherever through the pouring rain, but the car was dead silent aside from the sound of the rain bouncing off of the roof. The wipers moved back and forth, silently speeding up and slowing down with the speed of the raindrops.

"No. I was actually gonna let his ass live. Angelo made the decision before I could stop him." There was sadness in her voice and regret maybe. There were so many questions I wanted to ask her, but I had to be careful. Honey was hard to read and I didn't understand how Angelo was tied into all of this. It wouldn't be long before Keyshawn would wake up and notice I wasn't in the house and call the police. She wouldn't be able to get but so far if I could stall her.

I sighed, trying to sound empathetic. "Once again we are at the mercy of our men; they make all the decisions and our lives are either reactions or reflections of their choices." I waited. If Angelo controlled whether Rah died, maybe I could make Honey realize the situation she was in now was no different than the one she was in before, with a man controlling her, maybe even her money, her home.

"I ain't at the mercy of shit. No-damn-body is makin' these choices. I decided to get Rah out of prison. You'd think the nigga woulda said thanks or showed me some kinda gratitude. But no, he ain't even bother showin' me the respect of takin' his dick outta the bitch he was fuckin' when I walked in to meet him—in the house I decorated for him to come home to." A flash of lightning lit up the sky, illuminating her face. I could see tears silently trickling down her round cheeks and I lowered my head. At least we were getting somewhere. I was getting to her. I just needed to keep her talking.

"Honey, I hate to say it but Rasheed lived and was always led by his dick, not his brain. For as smart as he was all that shit would go out the window once the blood left his head and that piece of meat between his legs stiffened up. It ain't neva' matter how good I was to him or how faithful or how beautiful he thought I was. It took years of dealing with him for me to learn that. He almost died, almost lost everything including me, and havin' his son ain't wasn't even enough to

make him change, Honey." Glancing out the window I
tried to get my bearings, figure out where we were just
in case an opportunity presented itself where I could
bail out of the car.

"*You* wasted years because of him. Not me. I died
and I came back just for my daughter. The time I spent,
the pain I know, the shit I've seen was because of you
and Larissa and no one else. Y'all wrapped everyone
else up in y'alls plan to put him away. And what gave
y'all the right to decide I deserved to be put away too?
'Cause we was fuckin'? 'Cause me and Rah was in love
and you was the spiteful ass baby momma about to be
cast aside?"

My mind was on overdrive trying to come up with
something to diffuse the anger I could hear quickly
seeping into her voice. The last thing I wanted to do
was turn this into a power struggle between who deserved what punishment. We were wrong on many
levels and I lived with our decision every day, but now
wasn't the time to debate about that shit. Not with me
handcuffed on a road to who knews where and Honey
pissed the fuck off with a loaded gun.

"I didn't have anything to do with that, sweetheart.
That was all Larissa. When I knew what she'd done the
police already had you."

"Well you can talk that shit over with her when you
see her. As far as y'all are concerned I'm done; this shit
gonna end tonight and then I'm gonna get my daughter."

I was scared to even imagine Ris alive somewhere
being held all this time when I'd just assumed she'd
left us. *I could have had people out lookin' for her if I
hadn't just assumed the worst. Maybe we could have
found her.* My stomach was in knots at the thought
of seeing her, what I'd say, how much time we would

have, how Honey was gonna end this. I could see the signs for the pier in the distance and I knew this was pretty much it for me. I didn't know what's worse: knowing you're going to die or knowing that death was coming and not knowing *how* you're going to die.

I lowered my head and I started to pray. It was the only thing I could think to do. That's when I'd noticed it. The color made it stand out in bright contrast against the dark red and blue of my pajama top. I'd forgotten about the little pink card Keyshawn had given me, and tears filled my eyes as I slid it out of my pocket as quietly as possible, opening the little flap on the back, and pulling out the card.

> They told me my key to the city would unlock any lock, but you're the only one with the key to my heart—don't ever luse it. Keyshawn

I smiled at the typo; the poor thing was definitely an athlete and not a scholar. His words would have given me so much hope for a future and happiness and maybe even love. If only I'd have opened it when we were together, I could have said how I really felt. Instead I pressed the card to my lips, sending him a silent kiss. I was sliding the card back inside when I noticed something else. There was also a thin gold chain, attached to it a small gold skeleton key. I was scared to slide it over my neck; she might see it and take it from me. If I died I at least wanted to have it in my hand as close to me as possible.

"We almost there." She sounded cold and detached.

Glancing up I could see us pulling up to a loading dock of some sort. There were large storage containers all over the place, like the one Jim said they'd found Rasheed's body in. Panicking I tried to slide the gold

chain over my wrist so I wouldn't drop it, but my handcuffs were in the way. On a desperate whim, a spur-
of-the-moment thought, I glanced at the key and back
at the lock on the cuffs. *Skeleton keys are supposed
to be able to unlock any lock.* I looked up at Honey
to see if she was paying me any attention. Nervously,
hands shaking from the cold rain and adrenaline, I
jammed the little key into the lock and twisted. I held
my breath, squeezing my eyes closed tightly, thinking
the cuffs would just clink, unhinge, and fall off at any
second, and I could try to either roll out of the car or
jump Honey when she wasn't expecting it. When nothing happened I damn near broke down.

"You ready to be reunited with your wife? Lania said
y'all weren't gettin' along an' shit so I guess you can
thank me for makin' the "til death do you part' part of
your marriage happen so quickly."

I could feel myself giving up, or accepting my fate,
to put it in better words. Lania, Angelo . . . So far this
sounded like a bad joke and everyone in my life was in
on it except me. Rasheed, and possibly Larissa, were
both dead—it was starting to look like a bad dream
come true, and I just didn't understand or know Keyshawn's place or his role in any of it.

The car came to a stop. Maybe it was the way the
loading docks smelled or because I thought I was about
to die; I was feeling like a complete idiot. The one time
I decided to finally let someone else into my life they
managed to shred it completely apart. My stomach
was getting queasy, and I watched as Honey picked
up the gun from the passenger seat and started to get
out of the car. For some reason, even though it was
pretty much over for me, a sense of desperation set
in. I looked around, desperate for anything to help me
out. I even tried the key again, twisting it frantically

back and forth in both directions. I must've been turning the key in the wrong direction the first time. The lock on the cuffs clicked and they silently slid off. *Fuck. That's all the fuck I had to do?* I looked down, amazed that the key had worked. This was my chance, my last chance, probably the only opportunity I'd have at saving myself.

Honey was shielding herself from the rain as she got out to open the back door, ready to pull me out. I took that as my opportunity, and with the cuffs around my knuckles I pushed the door hard back at her, catching her off guard. Her feet slid in the mud and she fell backward.

The fact that I wasn't wearing any shoes worked to my advantage. I hopped out and dug my toes into the moist ground, giving myself better leverage as I lunged and climbed on top of her. Before she could raise her gun or get herself up, I hit her across the jaw. The inside of the cuffs cut into my skin and I ignored the pain shooting through my fist. I hit her three, four, five times, punching her repeatedly until the muscles in my arm started to shake and her body had gone limp, blood streaming from her nose and the corner of her mouth.

Searching her pockets I grabbed her cell, the pistol from her hand, and the keys to the car. I climbed into the driver's seat, intent on heading back to the house to get Trey and Taya and gettin' us the fuck out of town. *Damn.* Jim's cell number was programmed in my iPhone and of course I didn't have it memorized. If I could just get to the house, something in the contract had his number on it. He'd know a safe place for me to take the kids. It took me a few minutes to get used to the car's controls. I was flying in the direction of my house, hydroplaning on turns and curves, intent on getting myself there before Honey had another chance to finish me off.

Her phone started ringing from the seat beside me and my heart almost stopped beating in my chest when I saw Keyshawn's name. *Why is he calling Honey's phone? Should I answer it and let him know I'm okay? He gave me the key to my cuffs—obviously he wanted to help me. If I don't answer, what will he think had happened to me? What does he have planned for my children?* I couldn't risk it.

"Why are you calling this phone, Key?"

"Oh my God. No, Michelle! You didn't. What are you doing right now?" He sounded shocked and angry at hearing my voice, not the excitement I'd have expected hearing at me just barely escaping death.

"What am I doing? What the fuck are you doing, Keyshawn?"

"It's a lot to explain, baby. I've been helpin' keep you alive as much as possible without compromisin' myself. If you on Honey's phone I'm guessin' you in Honey's car?"

"Yeah. I used the key you gave me. In the envelope."

"*Fuck!*" Keyshawn rarely cursed and that one word scared the life out of me. *What did I "save" myself into?*

"Michelle, you gotta get out of that car, right now. Wipe your prints off the steering wheel and run from it. I'm packin' up some of your and the kids' things. I'm on my way to pick you up. I'll have the kids with me."

"Why? What's wrong, Key? You have to tell me." I pulled over to the side of the road and put the car into park. Using the bottom of my shirt I wiped the steering wheel. It was too late. I could see the red and blue lights comin' at me through the wind and rain. This bitch set me up.

"I didn't give you the key to use, Michelle; that's why when you set it down I ain't say nothin'. When I woke up and you were gone and it was gone . . ." His voice was drowned out by the sound of the sirens and the squad cars that surrounded me. That's when I realized he didn't spell "lose" wrong. He was trying to tell me not to use it. "Don't ever *luse* it." If I would've been thinking clearly maybe I would've picked up on that shit.

"Ma'am, get out of the car with your hands up." Slamming my hands up against the steering wheel I couldn't believe how stupid I'd been. If I'd have just run on foot I could have gotten away. That bitch anticipated my every fuckin' move just like I'd done with Rasheed, and like a mouse in a maze I'd blindly walked right into this brick wall, thinking it was a way out.

CHAPTER 29

IF YOU FAIL TO PLAN,
YOU PLAN TO FAIL

For half of a heartbeat I actually debated pushing the gas pedal to the floor and gunnin' it up out of there. I had no idea where I'd go or how far I'd get, but the image of every officer in the county opening fire and killing me before I could get more than a hundred yards away squelched the idea. I could only imagine the types of drugs Angelo and Honey would have stashed up in that damn car just to set my ass up—probably enough to put me away for life. Now I had an unregistered pistol with an illegal silencer on it in the passenger seat of a stolen car full of drugs, and no ID, with absolutely no logical explanation for any of it except that a woman who was supposed to have died in prison kidnapped me from my home at gunpoint and this was where I'd ended up. Yeah, I could see the cops believing that shit.

"Get on the ground now," someone yelled at me from somewhere in the rain. There were at least six different sets of high beams pointed in my direction, blinding me. I did as told. The cold, wet pavement scraped against my bare legs, rain ran into my eyes, for the second time in one night I was cuffed. A female officer grabbed my hands and forced them behind my back, almost pulling my arm out of the socket. I was pulled roughly to my feet and dragged over to stand beside one of the squad cars. Who knew what the hell Honey or whoever said when they called this bullshit in or how many drugs they told them I was carrying? I had an flashback of Rasheed being hauled out of his car and all I could think was that karma was definitely a complete and absolute fucking bitch.

One of the cops went through the glove compartment and came over to me with several pieces of paper in his hand. "Is there any reason why you're driving Mr. Curtis Daniels's vehicle, ma'am?"

I just stared at the officer blankly. No, I didn't have a damn reason. I was shocked—*why the fuck did Honey have Curtis's car?*

"Holy fuck, Miller. Come look at this shit!"

I was half pushed and half dragged toward the trunk of the car, where the other two officers were gathered. When my eyes finally landed on what they had back there that had them so in awe I almost fainted. They'd unzipped a large bag and the only thing I could make out was Curtis's body before gettin' sick. The smell of decaying flesh and the way he looked after being locked up in there decomposing in the heat for three or four weeks was unbearable. After that I was surrounded by pitch black. The haunting image of Larissa's face stuffed in the trunk underneath Curtis, the overwhelming smell of bodies, making everyone cover their mouths, fighting the urge to gag, her eyes dull and lifeless looking back at me, it was all more than I could handle at one time.

The smell of unwashed bodies and urine woke me up. I thought I was having a bad dream, that Honey and the car . . . everything was a bad dream. I opened my eyes. I was lying on a hard bunk, there was a toilet sticking out of the wall in front of me, and the realization set in that I was in a holding cell.

"Hello? Officer?" I looked out through the thin metal bars; there was a desk over in the corner but no one was there. Larissa's face . . . I couldn't get the image out of my head and I fought the urge to curl up in a ball and just cry. My clothes, well what little I'd had on, were taken from me and I was left in all-white cotton pants and a matching shirt.

"Look who's finally awake. Fuckin' Sleepin' Beauty over here." One of the officers walked in, eatin' pork rinds out of a bag, wiping the crumbs on his uniform. He was a pudgy pink-faced white man with a double chin that jiggled when he spoke.

"My name is Michelle Laurel, it used to be Michelle Roberts. I would like my one phone call please."

"Yeah, yeah, and motherfuckers in hell want ice water. You'll get your phone call when we ready to give you one."

"Stop fuckin' with her, Simmons, let her have her call." A female cop walked up, slappin' him playfully on his back. She was younger, probably about my age, brown skin, with friendly eyes.

"Can you look up a number for Jim Bartell please?"

Jim was the only person I could trust right now. She sat down at the desk for a moment, looking at her computer, before coming over to let me out, handing me the number on a Post-it note. She led me over to another room that looked like a cell, except it was surrounded with Plexiglas and had a phone in a center.

"I'm Officer James. Towanna James. Just let me know when you're done." She smiled at me and I liked her immediately.

I dialed Jim's number and almost cried when he answered. I was rambling and talking so fast, trying to tell him everything that'd happened literally overnight since he'd left that voice mail, it was a wonder he could keep up with me, but he did.

"This ain't as bad as you think, sweetheart. I'm sorry you're in there right now but be patient. Me and one of my boys will personally go by your place and pull all the security footage. I know you didn't commit them murders, sweet pea. I also record all of our conversations, so we have documented instances of you fearing for you and your late wife's lives. Our first suspect right now is gonna be that Honey woman, since she was the last person we saw Larissa alive with. It's a start and we'll go from there."

I hung up the phone, content that Jim would somehow work things out for me. I was confident that as long as the kids were with Keyshawn they were fine. Hopefully he'd grabbed enough Pull-Ups for Lataya to last a few days, and wherever he'd taken them, I just prayed it was someplace Honey and her people didn't know and couldn't find out about.

CHAPTER 30

AN UNMARKED MARKSWOMAN

"What the fuck, Honey?" Angelo was pacing back and forth lookin' like he was 'bout to burst a damn blood vessel. "Get the bitch, let her take the car. That was it. It was simple, so fuckin' simple."

"It was a mistake, she knocked me unconscious. I didn't know she'd take my gun."

Yes, we'd gone over the plan a million fuckin' times and had a million different scenarios. But not one included her whoopin' my ass with her handcuffs and takin' my damn pistol. We'd definitely underestimated little Miss "I'll Think You Into Some Shit Before I Beat You Into It," aka Michelle. I was still recovering from a broken nose, an' that bitch fractured the bone just beneath my fuckin' eye. I looked like I could be the poster child for spousal abuse.

"Yeah, but what the fuck have I always told you's? Neva', neva', leave your weapon or lay it down, right? I knew I shoulda went with you, sent someone with you."

I ain't answer. There was no point; he wasn't looking for no answer, he was just talkin' to hear himself talk right now and that was that.

"You my woman an' it's my job to protect you. I gotta figure out how to get us outta this city. We gonna have to lay low until this shit blow over."

"Ount need protectin', baby. I made a honest mistake an' I'ma fix this shit." We were sittin' up in one of Angelo's penthouses that was considered off the radar, one of his getaway spots for times like this when shit got too hot to be out on the streets. I was jus' sittin' my ass in one of the black ostrich recliners, starin' out through the huge floor-to-ceiling window in the sitting room at all the city lights that lit up Miami at night. From up here it looked like we owned this city, and somewhere down there, in spite of everything I'd planned, Michelle was still runnin' around a free woman.

"*Bella,* sweetie—you's got so much to learn. Up until that pistol *you* were the perfect weapon. A ghost, a ninja assassin, an unknown assailant who could strike anyone anywhere and vanish with no past and no file. You were untraceable. But now, they know you're out there, and they know you're gonna come back."

He had a point. I wanted to get Paris back and Michelle knew I would die before I let her keep my child. If Lania coulda controlled her damn nigga we would not have had half of this problem. I went to Michelle's house afterward but Keyshawn's ass was gone. He'd taken Trey and Paris to who knew where and hadn't been seen since. I got up and walked into the bathroom.

"We not done talkin'; where you goin'?"

"I'll be right back, Angelo."

Walkin' into the penthouse bathroom was like goin' into a damn mini spa. Heated marble floors, crystal knobs on all the Koehler faucets, I was gettin' used to havin' the best of everything. I turned the water on, watchin' it swirl around the crystal bowl basin. I looked at myself in the mirror. *When did I become this woman, this rich man's canary to be kept in a cage— this bloodthirsty killer?* It was like I was living a double life.

The real me was hidin' away somewhere deep down inside, waitin' until the all clear was announced so she could come back out. *I should have done this shit a long time ago.* Reachin' into the medicine cabinet I grabbed a razor blade from Angelo's shaving kit and some alcohol to sterilize the blade. Trenisha's past was what got me caught up and I needed to erase that bitch once and for all.

"Angel face, you all right in there or what?" Angelo was knockin' on the door but at this point I couldn't open it. The shit hurt worse than I thought it would and shock and too much fuckin' pain was going through my arms for me to even move from where I was sittin' on the side of the tub to let him in.

"Honey? You good? What's goin' on in there?" He kicked the door open; wood splintered around the lock, and I looked up at him, teary eyed, tryin' not so fuckin' hard not to let him see me cry.

"I erased her, Angelo. There ain't no more Trenisha. There ain't no more Honey. That shit won't ever happen again."

"Fuck, woman, what the fuck did you do?"

Blood was all over me, it was all over the bathroom floor. He knelt in front of me and held up my bloody hands. I'd taken the razor blades and sliced the fingerprints clean off of my fingers one by one, cutting deep enough to where there were now only bloody pads where my skin used to be.

"No more mistakes, Angelo. I promise."

"Oh my God. Let me see. What made you do this shit?" He snatched his shirt off and grabbed my hands and started wrapping them up in it, trying to stop the blood.

I winced because it stung, but didn't pull my hands back.

"We gonna get my daughter. I don't care where I have to go or what else I have to do. All I want is my daughter."

"Yeah, Honey, we gonna get our princess I promise. On my life, I swear we'll get her back." He kissed my forehead, smoothing my hair back, and I drifted into sleep or passed out, I wasn't sure which. But my last thoughts were of a beautiful little baby girl with golden skin and chubby cheeks. Smiling at me though long, curly-ass lashes, it was a smile I'd seen a million times and I felt as though I hadn't seen that smile in a million years—it was my smile.

CHAPTER 31

WHEN IT ALL COMES DOWN

All the shit Honey and Angelo put me through to get me locked up and not one ounce of it could stick. Jim went to the DEA and all the charges against me were dropped within a week. The pistol that was used to murder Larissa was also the same gun used to kill Rasheed. There was no way I could have been in Virginia at the time he was murdered and when they ran the gun through forensics they found a second set of prints along with mine that belonged to Trenisha, also known as Honey. They did an autopsy on Curtis's body and his estimated time of death placed me at Chuck E. Cheese with the kids. They even pulled the photos from the hard drive in the booth from that day to help verify I couldn't have been the person to stab him and then cut off his arm.

It was such a relief to be treated like a normal member of society again. They'd reopened Honey's case to determine how someone declared dead could be walking around committing murders. Honey was on all the bulletins and wanted ads; they had an older picture from her first prison arrest but it was a close enough resemblance for someone to identify her, and it did not surprise me at all that she'd suddenly vanished off the face of the earth along with Angelo and Lania.

With Honey and Angelo in hiding I was anxious to find Keyshawn and the kids. I'd asked Jim to pick me up a new phone since I'd dropped mine, and even though he was watching the house, I was still too scared to go back to that place. I dialed Keyshawn's number.

"Michelle?" he answered, and I could hear the kids screaming for me in the background.

I breathed a sigh of relief. "Yeah, it's me. They let me go. Honey fucked up and had her prints on the gun. I guess she wasn't expecting me to grab it, but combined with the footage from my home surveillance and Jim's security info to back me up they didn't have anything to tie me to the murders. I had an alibi and they had no material evidence. We even got records of Larissa's calls to Lania the day she disappeared."

I could hear the stress in his voice. I could only think what he was going through tryin' to keep up with two kids. "I'm so sorry. I tried to keep you and the kids safe for as long as I could, Michelle. Angelo's my half brother by marriage so goin' against him would have caused major shit with the family. I had to do whatever I could to keep me safe and pray you would still make it out of there okay. I had no idea why they wanted to get to you; all I knew is Lania and Angelo's new woman had it out for you since the day we met to look at that property, and, as part of the family, I either went with them or I was automatically against them."

I had to give Honey credit, she'd set this shit up damn near flawlessly. If I hadn't had the foresight to grab her gun after I'd knocked her unconscious there wouldn't be any reasonable doubt to stop them from pressing full double homicide charges against me.

"I wanna see my babies, Key. I miss you guys so much. Where are you?"

"Meet me at the spot where we first met. You already know Trey and Taya been missin' you something terrible. I have been too."

I was still paranoid as hell and I called Jim to make sure I wasn't being followed before I left the hotel I was staying in. I sent someone ahead to scope out the only place I could think of that Keyshawn could have meant. After getting the all clear from Jim I rented a car and went to see my babies, all of them. As I pulled into the circular driveway I couldn't help but notice the place was just as I remembered it; not a hedge, leaf, or stone was out of place. So much of our heartache started all because of this property, and I couldn't help seeing the irony in the fact that here I was once again, right back at square one.

"Momeeeeeeee."

Tears streamed down my cheeks as I knelt down to hug Trey. There was a point when I thought I'd never see my son again; looking into his bright eyes and kissing his smiling face filled me with so much joy.

"I'm so glad you made it out of all this okay." Keyshawn walked out of the back door holding Lataya in his arms. They both had the biggest grins on their faces.

Standing, I couldn't hide anything as I walked over to kiss them both. I felt at peace and there was so much love in my heart for Keyshawn. No matter what doubts I'd ever had about him or where our relationship would go, he'd saved my children for me and I'd always owe him my undying gratitude for that.

"So what do we do now?" I looked at him still holding Lataya and tried to figure out how we could still make it out of this and salvage something from our relationship.

"We leave Florida. Angelo and Honey gonna be lyin' low for a minute. Lania's pretty much wanted right now for her connection to Larissa goin' missing. I say we see what Cali is like, or Maryland."

I understood what he meant but I couldn't see me running from yet another situation. "I say, we like Florida, and we stay right here. You keep playin' ball for the Legends and I'll keep doing what I do. When they come for us, *if* they come for us, we'll be ready."

"So you wanna stay right here? Right in the middle of Angelo's stompin' ground?"

"Keyshawn, what good is leaving gonna do if they'll follow us wherever we go? If Angelo gonna send men out to wherever we are? We'll be runnin' our entire lives."

He handed me Lataya and was looking at me in disbelief, like he couldn't imagine me wanting to stay in Florida. "I can't do that shit, Michelle. I was supposed to take Honey her daughter that night and put Trey back on a plane to Virginia. They both probably want me dead. If not now then they will as soon as they've realized that I ain't do what I was s'posed to do."

"So what are you telling me, Key?" Looking him in his eye I dared him to tell me he was gonna leave me, standing right there with my son and my daughter like we weren't shit after all we'd been through together. I couldn't see it happening. But he didn't need to tell me anything. Kissing me on my forehead, he turned and walked toward his car.

I couldn't believe this nigga was walkin' out on us like this, but I expected it. These weren't his kids, I wasn't his wife, and he had his own problems to deal with. Grabbing Trey's hand I walked into this new, cold, empty house. It was time for us to start over. No drama, no bullshit, no ghosts, and no craziness. I didn't need anyone else to help me with my kids. I could and I would do this all on my own.

CHAPTER 32

MIGHT AS WELL GO OUT WITH A BANG

"Where's Uncle Key goin', Mommy?" Trey asked me quietly.

I fought the tears and the heartache; I needed to be stronger than what I thought possible. "He's going home, baby."

I'd barely closed the back door when I was knocked off my feet. All the air whooshed out of my body in one painful breath. Trey yelled and Lataya wailed.

"Trey, go upstairs! Take your sister upstairs!" I rolled onto my side, clutching my stomach as he scampered away, half dragging his crying sister behind him.

"How did I know this is where he'd meet you? Of all the places, he'd have you come here."

Lania was standing above me, her eyes wild with fury and hate. She glared down at me, shotgun in hand—muzzle to the ground. She was leaning on it like a crutch, slightly swaying back and forth.

"All he did was bring me my kids, Yylannia. There's nothing to us. You want him, you got him."

She sneered down at me. "You can't give me what's already mine, bitch. He's so damn caught up with your ass he's willing to die. I'm not worried about you. I just need the little girl so Angelo will let me and Key live in peace."

The meaning behind her words was all too clear. I slowly struggled to sit. No one was going to touch my daughter and the thought alone ignited a fire in my soul.

"You're going to have to kill me to get her. Is all of this really worth it? Do you think it's going to be that easy?" I glanced around, looking for something, anything to use in defense.

"Oh, Chelly. Poor Chelly. Misguided, thinks-she-owns-the-world little Chelly. I can do whatever the fuck I want, bitch! Angelo's my brother, sweetheart. We own Miami." She laughed, and it was the most deranged-sounding witch's cackle I'd ever heard in my life.

I watched helplessly as she raised the barrel of the shotgun. My mind was going berserk. I tried calculating how much time I'd have to stand and lunge or roll to the side. *Can I even make it to her before she pulls the trigger?* I didn't have a choice; my babies were not going to see me laid out in this floor.

"Stand the fuck up and take this shit like a woman. I'd hate to have to tell everyone I killed a cowering bitch."

Slowly I dragged myself upright. I didn't plan it and I sure as hell didn't fully think it through. I lunged at Lania's feet. The sound of the shotgun momentarily deafened me and she screamed as the bullet smashed through the door behind me. I didn't give her a chance to get any kind of leverage on that shotgun. I hit her in the jaw so hard I was sure my hand was broken.

Nothing prepares you for those split-second moments. They happen faster than lightning and you are all instinct and reaction. Before Lania could react I'd grabbed the gun, stood, and before I could think about consequences or anything else I fired. I hit her center mass—square in the chest. Shotgun still in hand I ran to get Trey and Lataya. They were hunkered together on the bottom of the stairs, crying hysterically.

"It's okay, babies. I promise everything is okay. Let's go get in the car."

I led them around Lania's body, turning their heads into my leg so they wouldn't look. There was a hole the size of tennis ball in the back door and the light from the sun cast a lonely ray through it. I turned the handle and nothing could stop the scream that escaped me. Nothing could have prepared me for what I saw and my heart split in two as tears streamed from my eyes. I dropped the shotgun and knelt down.

Keyshawn was lying outside the door. I already knew he was gone. His eyes stared unblinking toward the sky and blood covered his chest. He was still holding a bouquet of flowers in his left hand. *God, he must have reconsidered what I said and decided to come back.* There was so much bloodshed surrounding me and all of it was because of Rasheed and his hoing-ass ways. I was tempted to dig his body up from wherever it was buried and shoot him again, several times, just for all the pain we were going through.

I didn't know where I got the strength from but I stood. The kids were still beside me; their little scared faces would probably scar me for life. Kissing my fingers I touched Keyshawn's eyes and closed them.

"You two okay?" I asked quietly.

I looked at my babies, and I knew for a fact Honey wouldn't stop until I was dead and Lataya was back with her. I called the police and waited in my rental car for them to arrive. Officer Towanna, the one who helped me, was the first one to get there.

"Michelle, right? You all right?" She approached me with her weapon drawn.

"I'm good. You won't be needin' that gun though, they ain't gonna move."

She radioed for backup and smiled reassuringly. "Well, you sure do seem to keep a lot of drama surrounding your ass."

I smiled at her attempt to ease the tension. After I explained everything that had happened, Towanna offered to personally escort me and the kids to a new hotel while everything was being investigated. She didn't trust anyone else, since Lania and Angelo were known to pay off police officers and at the moment I didn't trust *anyone*.

"Y'all need me, you have my card and my cell phone number." She was standing at the doorway to the hotel room.

"Thank you for everything, Offi . . . Towanna. I just want a hot bath and sleep right now."

I watched as she closed the door and it felt as though a chapter was closing. My heart had been ripped out, replaced, and ripped out again, and I had no idea how to rebuild it this time. Every fiber in my body was screaming for me to just break down. I wanted to scream, cry, crawl into a hole, and never come out. There was now a gaping wound in my heart and nothing aside from my kids would ever be able to fill it again.

Everyone close to me was gone. It was just me and my two little ones, and if Honey wouldn't stop until I was dead . . . well, then it only made sense for me to try to kill her first. She'd made this game strictly life or death, and above all else I was choosing life.